death
and
so
forth

also by gordon lish

death
and
so
forth

a tisket of twenty scriptions

by
gordon
lish

DZANC BOOKS

DZANC
BOOKS

5220 Dexter Ann Arbor Rd.
Ann Arbor, MI 48103
www.dzancbooks.org

First US edition: April 2021
Interior design by Michelle Dotter

Library of Cngress Cataloguing-in-Publication Data available upon request.

Printed in the United States of America

10   9   8   7   6   5   4   3   2   1

Regeleh! Pheewee! Fishky! Neni! Meyer! Please!

The author thanks Roberto Casati
and Achille C. Varzi for invaluable
considerations involving the formation
and, accordingly, deformation of holes,
hollows, cavities, hosts, circumflictions,
and circumflexes. Ah, let us hear no fewer huzzahs
for Jeremy Davies, bold tout in a piercing rain.

How surely the dead are beyond death.

—Cormac McCarthy

CONTENTS

DEATH AND SO FORTH

WORD IN FRONT

Ordinarily—hah, is there ever anything legit coming to you when the pitchman opens with "Well, folks, uh, ordinarily" . . . ? You know, or should know, there's every reason to expect there's mostly malarkey on the way.

Or how about hooey?

Except, yeah, this is really aulde Gordo sitting here at his really aulde Underwood speaking to you, and, even if I slipped up and let the word ordinarily inaugurate my spiel, I ask that in the case of this ultra-particular swindle, you go along with me for a while, make believe I'm perfectly innocent of any intent to set you up for a fast one, any self-aggrandizing, or, say, some smarm of face-saving up my sleeve.

Sound phony?

Fake?

Because, golly, boys and girls, the wearying fact is that a goodsome share of the motive informing my diction was to investigate my competence to check if I could still spell ordinarily correctly.

Or even get it close enough.

Sound plausible?

Or like a loathsome dodge?

Especially when you might not be unaware of the putative writer-in-charge having spent years as an undisputed editor-in-charge, at *Genesis West, Esquire*, Alfred A. Knopf, *The Quarterly*—plus, ugh, in the classroom and, ugh, as a teacher.

You see, the thing all of a sudden is that I, Gordo, have begun to discover myself at a scary and scarier distance from my feeling much sure-footed anymore, right up, for instance, to the instant ago when I started to stumble into a worry pit beset with wonderment: As per, hold it, um, that bit supposed to fit the situation, is it anymore or any more?

Are you buying this?

Buy it.

I'm making an admission.

Because here's the thing of it, as the poet says—the entries up ahead, these importunings all alert to your prospective collaboration, they may indeed be no better than a horde of horrors (love it, that alliterizing; am just, oh boy, every so often, helpless to exhibit myself as other than its gleeful victim), but for true, for true, they're, the pieces, these collected, these selected pieces, up there on their tippy-toes, standing at brightsome, hopeful, heartfelt attention in an expectant, well-groomed row—well, they unhappily happen to have slumping among them (here it comes, the shameless shamstering, the unregenerate huckster doubling back behind your back and pitching his shuck just when you were beginning to sense yourself more or less suckered into a spirit of succumbent forgiveness—pitiless, oh pitiless, the bullshit artist!—letting yourself take the dirty dickens at his word).

Oh, heavens, his word!

Horseplay?

Up on the back of his hobbyhorse hobbling his hoy up and down the page.

No, no, my friend, this is an honest man's preparation for confession, his implorement for your conceding, or, anyhow, entertaining the charity of an apportioned concession.

A pleading, that's what I'm making. I'm finagling like mad to make amends for an exception, a remission of judgment, your mercy cast into the immersion of a mutuality beginning not impossibly to erupt profitably between us.

You see, time was when I was seated here at the Underwood and the product of my keeping company with a machine was a bit I titled, or entitled, heart high with pride, "Excelsior." Thereafter, given my being a faithful confederate of Bob Fogarty, editor of *The Antioch Review*, I slip "Excelsior" in the mail to him and, in the evil between-time of real-time experience, it returns to me in print and I, not yet heartsore, still all heart and pretty expectation, I go scurrying off to sit myself down under an interior tree here in the house, to glory over offspring with (what ho!) vastly more worn-down eyes—and, jeepers, golly willikers, more than mildly—indeed, I was, well, downright insanely, I guess I should murmur—astonished.

As in I. Wrote. This. Crap?

Etc., etc.—or, if it redresses any balance—&c., &c.

Fine.

I'll fix it, okay?

Consult with the Underwood and unmess the mess, yes?

Yet (ouch!) time and tide—and all the rest of what notoriously undoes our doings—pass, have passed, and (whoops) all of a sudden swept me into a past plucking a string in the word pasture.

Uh-oh.

Once younger Gordo is now older and older and older Gordo.

Indeed, as try after try at unmessing matters commences to make clearer to me: I am all of a sudden a Gordo gone too far into what remains, or, worse, remained, of his Gordonness. Gee, the capper of the famous progress is—as we each of us will all of us be made to reckon with in the course of our various courses—agh, history.

So you say fine, tough luck, you lived too long, buddy, cut the piece and cut the crap and ship the remainder off to Dzanc, repairing to your diminishing interior resources, take a nap, maybe take your sleeping pills a lot earlier tonight, hit the sack before you can't feel along the wall and furniture to it, and, like a mensch, face the age-old face of things and call it a day.

Mmm?

But pay attention.

I can't. Couldn't. Won't. Wouldn't. Shall not.

No, no, not for me the stiff upper-lippery demanded of the geriatric citizen, for I am no less the Gordo, hapless nephew once adrift in the war-torn 1940s, whose Uncle Charlie and Aunt Dora never for a sec ever let the boy down.

Not on your life would I them!

Not when it was their presence in my hell-bent truancy that made me measure myself against an example meriting (yeah!) adoration and (yeah, you bet!) imitation.

Look, the geezer-in-charge is shouting at you—not one arthritic finger would he struggle to lift and press upon the keyboard of his trusty Underwood to ex out (as in xxxxxxxxxxx) "Excelsior."

Are you hearing this?

The more I fumbled around with things, futzing and futzing with every phoneme, working myself up into a state of nutsier and nutsier nutsiness, the more did there emerge a reemergence (vide the rearmost page in this book) worser and worser.

My friend (are we still not on affirmative terms?), the sorry bobble remains in place, awaiting your mercy, your humanity, your rachmones (oh, go ask somebody, I'm busy composing a sentence)—well, your, you know, words to the register of the swindler's earnest beseechment.

Me?

No discomposure, I swear it, just resignation loudly acknowledged—and a hearty greeting to you called out to you from the gatherment of shadow.

Welcome.

Well may you fare.

Whether you are a writer or a reader or, not unlikely, both, have some fun while you're at it—until you can't.

JAWBONE

Not to worry. You mustn't worry. There were only two of them. Look at it this way—they were courting. That's the story for you—courting, sure. Didn't I tell you already? I think I told you already—grayish, silvery—a silvery grayishness. Please, you're blowing this all out of proportion, or is it out of all proportion that you're blowing it? Don't blow it like that, okay? Anyway, two, I said only two—I got them both—first one, then the other. Like how else, you know? You know what I'm saying? My God, did they run. But I got them, goddamn it, the fucking filthinesses. Calm down. The thing to do is to be very calm. See the sport in it if you can. No, I don't suppose they could have gone all the way yet. Conceiving—that kind of thing. Multiplying. Right, right, I got them one at a time. They had to have already like, you know, split. Oh, you never saw speed like this kind of speed—outrunning their glamour and racing in different directions. So that wasn't so easy for anyone who's half asleep, was it? Had to really hustle. Had to look sharp, you know? With my hand? God no. With the roll—with the toilet paper roll, with the standby roll we've been keeping at the ready in there—bam, bam—like that. Splat. Come on, I'm kidding, I'm just kidding. There was no splat. My God, there was nothing to them. No innards, not even either one of them dead with a shell. Take it easy. Look, see the achievement in it, can't you see the achievement?—it's the middle of the night, they're there in the bathroom, a pair of bugs not even coupling. Oh, Jesus, knock it off. You're being ridiculous. No, I can't show you, you don't want to see—the whole saga of it got deposited into the garbage hours ago—Jesus, just two spots not any bigger than a minute apiece. But dark ones—absolutely. Not so grayishly silveryish anymore. Well, I'm giving you the facts. Turned on the light, sat down on the toilet seat—because me, I'm all set to read, right? Then there's this feeling of the thereness of it even before you're even seeing it. You know, the sense of there is something out of place, a difference in the format? That's the word, those are the words, take any of them—shift, format, change. Lord God, a prescience, I'm calling it, something off, a thing awry there in the given space. Bam, bam! Thank God we keep that backup roll ready to rock and roll when it's time for the canonical shits in there—there, as they say, in the can. Oh, now quit it, will you? Will you just please relax? A couple of kibitzers, for pity's god-damn sake. Wise guys. Perps. Theater types. They was asking for it, so I gives it to 'em. Not bam, bam—more like bam bam. Com-maless. Listen, honey, let's cut the crap with the commas—a case like this, operators going and getting all crazy touchy, what choice does a copper got? Oh, hey, darn—enough already, okay? All I'm doing is seeing we inject some perspective into the thing. Yes, a grayish kind of lucent effect—a little shiny, if that's what lucent means—until I slapped the fucking lucence right the fuck out of them, didn't I? No, no—you can go ahead and check the bin if you want, but I'm telling you, it'll just be blood and guts, is all. Look, I'm horsing around with you, can't you tell? Please, can't a person horse around with another person? Like lucky thing for the local citizenry someone on your side was in there on duty on the nightbeat last night there in the crapper, right? Yes, yes, they're utterly thoroughly gone to glory, you can bank on it. Blots. Dots. Snip, pip—but, you know, what's ever anywhere near snipped and pipped enough? Okay, hyphenate it all you want if that's what's sensible in a summary like this. Snip-pip in one sense, yes, positively yes—yet really in truth more like it's all in the register of the vowels, full stop, wham! Death on a tile floor. Or is it, do you say, tiled? Anyway, a pair of grout-eaters probably. Out grazing in the dark and starstruck as all get-out—until they go and get themselves gobsmacked for their bother and trouble and sex-madness, or is it trouble and bother and so on? No real romance in it, nothing like the duet of long-nappers the mixed metaphor, the whole oratorio, drawls when it drawls us. Just a yawning deficit, pests asunder. Ho-hum, we're dead. Hey, they, I said they, them. Can't you see the symmetry in it? But you're right, all right. Incident, cognition—oops, too late, finito, it's finished, what's narrable's been narrated, not even life enough left for the vacant feeling famous on paper. Behold instead the ghastly presentiment present and as yet unaccounted for in, you know, in the tummy of your overfed insect. The weight of grout—et cetera and et cetera. Ugh. But we mustn't dwell on it. Weren't there only the two of them? Light, the light!—run, won't you? Quick—make for anything vertical! You bet, it's definitely curtains, but—goddamn it, goddamn it—is hopeless flight never not noticed?—at least anyway, by anyway at least by the hopeful? Sweetheart, just don't you pay any of it any mind. It's all of it just a displacement in that format thing I've just been telling you about—it's all just a feeling in the night, right up until a roll of personal tissue probably comes into it—or maybe even some other household product. Well, fuck, bugs—I mean, what can anyone—us, for instance—really do?

NAUGAHYDE

He said, "You know what I think of when I think of us?"

She said, "Tell me."

He said, "The chair."

She said, "Us in the chair."

"You with your leg up," he said.

"My left leg," she said.

He said, "Right. I mean, your left leg—right."

She said, "I'll think about this tonight."

"The chair?" he said. "Our time in the chair?"

"No," she said. "The way you said it," she said.

He said, "How I said it was how it came to me to say."

She said, "Nothing just comes. It's all rehearsed."

He said, "You think that's the way we are?"

"It's not what I think," she said. She said, "It's what is. Or was," she said.

"Take it back," he said.

"Look," she said, "I have to get off," she said.

He said, "Sorry. I wanted to talk."

"More past tense," she said.

He said, "You listen too closely."

She said, "Wasn't that the thrill?"

"Of course," he said. "It had its charms. Everything known," he said.

She said, "So it seemed."

"Not just talk," he said. "Everything else," he said. "Nothing not given."

"Hang up," she said.

"Exactly," he said.

•

"Hi," he said.

She said, "Okay, have it your way."

"That's funny," he said. He said, "You know what?"

"Tell me what," she said.

He said, "You're still funny," he said.

"Nothing funny about this," she said.

"Don't you mean *that*?" he said.

"I mean you're calling too often," she said.

He said, "Can't seem to help it. You want me to help it?" he said.

"Make an effort," she said.

He said, "You think I'm not making an effort?"

"Make more of one," she said.

"Yeah," he said. "You're right," he said. "But I close my eyes and I see the chair," he said.

"Cut it out," she said. "Who has to close them?" she said. She said, "It's not right where it was? You're impossible," she said.

He said, "Yeah." He said, "Nothing's changed." He said, "Everything's right where it was."

She said, "Get off the phone, please."

He said, "Make me."

She said, "I'm hanging up."

"Who's stopping you?" he said.

"Oh, for God's sake," she said.

"All right," he said. "I think I hear her anyway."

"Give her my best," she said. "Look," she said, "if you're so dying to talk about the chair, talk to her about it," she said.

"Hang up," he said.

She said, "Consider it done."

"I'm waiting," he said.

"Enough," she said. "Don't call," she said.

He said, "I'll think about it." He said, "I'm thinking about it." He said, "Did I say it's right in this room?"

"You said you hear her," she said. "For everybody's sake, hang up," she said. She said, "Please, I'm getting off."

"Fine," he said. "Get off," he said.

•

He said, "How nice of you to call."

She said, "This a bad time?"

"It's a safe time," he said. "Been thinking?" he said.

"Never not," she said.

"Fine and dandy," he said.

"That's nice," she said.

He said, "Nice." He said, "It's nice when it's nice."

She said, "Are we remembering it as it was?" She said, "That's not possible, is it?" She said, "But it was nice, very nice," she said.

"Couldn't have been nicer," he said.

"The chair," she said.

"Right," he said.

"That's all I wanted to say," she said. "But call me," she said. "When it's safe," she said.

He said, "Of course."

"Yes," she said. "Of course," she said.

●

"I remember things," she said.

"The chair?" he said.

"Didn't she have it recovered?" she said.

"Reupholstered," he said.

She said, "Mmm." She said, "Nothing stays the same."

"That's deep," he said.

"There's no reason to be mean," she said.

"Right you are," he said. "You know what?" he said. He said, "You're right." He said, "But not everything does," he said.

She said, "What?"

He said, "Change."

"Oh, God," she said.

"Yeah, sure," he said.

She said, "Tell me what you remember."

"You tell me first," he said.

"This is awful," she said.

He said, "You're telling me."

She said, "Uh-oh. Hanging up."

●

"Are we thinking?" she said.

"Let's think," he said.

"Let's fuck," she said.

He said, "Christ. Christ," he said.

"My thought is this," she said. "My thought is it's impossible to think," she said. She said, "My thought is it's better if we quit calling."

"Okay," he said.

"Okay," she said.

•

"You want to hear my thought?" he said.

"We agreed," she said.

"Nothing doesn't change," he said.

She said, "Which of us said that?"

"Too deep for it to have been me," he said.

"Is she there?" she said.

"Out," he said.

She said, "At the upholsterer's or at the reupholsterer's?"

He said, "How would you like it if I said at chemo?"

"Say it," she said. "Go ahead and say it," she said. She said, "You think everyone doesn't die?"

"I think we'll die," he said.

"Who's not already dying?" she said. She said, "When are we not dying?"

"We were alive," he said.

"We were," she said. "It felt like we were really alive," she said.

He said, "Say as if," he said.

"As if," she said.

•

He said, "Are we making this up?"

She said, "What other course is there?"

He said, "Then we're lucky for that."

She said, "Lucky how?"

"That we can," he said.

"That one wants to," she said.

He said, "There's no out-talking you."

She said, "Oh yes, there is."

"I think I hear her," he said.

"She's not dead?" she said.

"Is he?" he said.

•

He said, "You remember what it was covered with?"

She said, "How couldn't I?"

He said, "Then tell me how it was."

"This a test?" she said.

He said, "What isn't?"

"Pity the pedestrians on the esplanade," she said.

He said, "You don't remember, do you?"

She said, "Am I the expert in what I remember?" She said, "I have all I can do to remember how to spell it anymore." She said, "You think I haven't forgotten your name sometimes?"

He said, "But then you remember it."

She said, "I sometimes remember your phone number sooner than I do your name." She said, "It was rose-colored or something." She said, "Velvet maybe."

He said, "Likelier velveteen."

"Lovely," she said.

"Lovely," he said.

She said, "The word, I mean."

"The word," he said. "To be sure."

•

"It wasn't that," he said.

"What? What," she said, "are you talking about?" she said.

He said, "What it was covered with," he said.

"In," she said.

"Okay, in," he said.

"You know what I'm wondering?" she said.

"Tell me what you're wondering," he said.

She said, "Tell me why it was I who provided the sheet."

"The bedsheet?" he said.

"Yes," she said. "I'd like to know how come it was always me who did. It was your place," she said. "How come was it that it was always I?" she said. She said, "What was the strategy with that?" she said.

"What a word," he said.

"Strategy?" she said.

He said, "Jesus, that's the worst word I ever heard come out of your mouth."

She said, "Did it never occur to you the chance I was taking?" She said, "What were you thinking when it was all me all of the time who was taking the biggest risk?"

"Bigger," he said. "Better to have said bigger," he said.

"Good God," she said.

"Exactly," he said. He said, "I'm tired." He said, "I think I'm tired," he said. He said, "I'm sorry—I'm going to go take a nap."

"Then go," she said.

He said, "Yeah, I think I must."

She said, "Fine. He's due any second now anyway."

"I'll phone," he said,

She said, "Yes, of course. You do that," she said.

●

He said, "Why this tack to harden yourself?"

"It's working," she said. "I'm harder," she said.

"Think what you're doing," he said.

She said, "Think? Who thinks?" she said.

"Oh, Jesus—please," he said.

She said, "That was the car. Goodbye," she said.

●

She said, "He read me something this morning."

He said, "The latest from Hallmark?"

She said, "A bit from one of the journals he gets."

"I'm all ears," he said.

"He's no lout, you know," she said.

"I'm all apologies," he said.

"This is childish," she said.

"I said I'm sorry," he said.

She said, "Try to put your back into it," she said.

He said, "I'm listening. Go ahead," he said.

She said, "That no matter the woman—"

He said, "Oh, this is going to be deeply deep," he said.

She said, "There's a man who's weary of her."

"That's it?" he said.

"That's not enough?" she said.

"Pretty profound," he said.

She said, "There's a point there." She said, "Don't you think there's a point there?"

He said, "It applies all around," he said. "Try this," he said. "Try no matter the person," he said.

She said, "We'll speak another time."

He said, "Talk now."

"Not in the mood," she said.

He said, "Oh, begging the lady's pardon, a mood, is it, then?"

She said, "I'm saying goodbye."

He said, "So say it."

"Goodbye," she said.

•

"Hi," he said.

She said, "I think he's in the house."

He said, "It happens I know for a fact she is."

"Then let's not either of us risk it," she said.

He said, "Are you forgetting what we risked?"

She said, "I'm not comfortable," she said. "This is unintelligent," she said. "We're asking for trouble," she said.

"Fine," he said. "Let's let comfort be our aim."

She said, "Call when you're thinking straight."

He said, "All right, I will."

"Then do it," she said.

•

"I miss you," he said.

"Oh," she said, "so much missing, so much missing, so much missing."

He said, "Don't worry, there's plenty more where that came from."

She said, "Who'd ever imagine?"

He said, "That we die, that we're dying, that we're every minute less alive." He said, "It's not slipped your mind, has it?"

"Not for a fucking instant," she said.

"Let's talk about the chair," he said.

She said, "How about the floor, how about the bed?"

He said, "I shouldn't have called."

"On the contrary," she said.

"Then hello," he said. He said, "I believe I said I miss you."

She said, "Aren't we at our best on the phone?"

"Good for you," he said. "Getting more callous by the day."

"Look," she said, "this isn't a very good time," she said.

He said, "Oh, yeah—time," he said.

"Just say goodbye," she said.

"Perfect," he said. "Perfectamundo," he said. "Goodbye," he said.

She said, "Another time."

"Oh, positively," he said. He said, "There'll come a time," he said.

"Next time," she said.

●

"It just so happens he reads Agamben," she said.

He said, "What's that?"

"Never mind," she said.

He said, "No, I'm interested," he said. "This is the kind of thing that really interests me," he said.

"What does she read?" she said.

He said, "Don't know." He said, "She's secretive about it. Hides her books," he said. "Burns them," he said. "Donates them to the starving," he said. "Thinks reading's capitalism's last stand."

"This is beneath us," she said.

He said, "Speak for yourself," he said.

She said, "She doesn't really have cancer," she said. "Does she?" she said.

"Thinks she does," he said.

"Thinks what?" she said.

"Cancer," he said. "All varieties," he said. "Just another one," he said, "of, you know," he said, "one of capitalism's last stands," he said.

She said, "Was the chair beneath us?"

He said, "The floor, the bed."

"The bedsheet on the floor," she said. "The bedsheet on top of the bedsheet on top of the bed," she said. "My bedsheet," she said.

"True enough," he said. He said, "Yours." He said, "Never one of mine," he said.

"Mine to wash," she said.

"True enough again," he said. "Yours to take home and wash," he said. He said, "Any more exposition called for?"

"We had something," she said.

He said, "Don't we still?"

"Yes—death," she said.

He said, "But until death?"

She said, "Is that a question?"

He said, "An invitation. A solicitation. A dare."

"Rhymes with chair," she said.

"Hell," he said, "does Agamben somewhere get to that?"

She said, "You'd do well to do as well."

He said, "Very nice. Anything else?" he said.

"I'm thinking," she said.

"Ah, rehearsing, is it?" he said.

She said, "Want to drop all this?"

He said, "All what?"

"Oh, please," she said. "Can't you grow up?" she said.

He said, "You know how old I am?"

She said, "It's hopeless." She said, "You're hopeless."

"That's not how you felt on the chair," he said.

"You want to know what I felt on the chair?" she said.

He said, "Make it good and hard and tough and mean and as callous as you can. Show me your stuff," he said. "Do unto me as you did unto me on the chair," he said.

She said, "Since you asked."

He said, "Oh, go ahead. Didn't I ask?"

She said, "Next time." She said, "He's coming."

"Always another time," he said.

"That's right," she said. "We live with other people," she said.

"We die with them," he said.

"We die alone," she said.

●

She said, "Didn't you say she redid the chair?"

He said, "We talked about it." He said, "You can't have forgotten we talked about it," he said. He said, "The chair, the carpeting, the plumbing, the viaduct, the forests in the Sudan." He said, "Years ago. She recovered everything," he said.

She said, "With what?"

He said, "Don't know." He said, "A sort of leather-like thing. But maybe not," he said. He said, "I'll take a look and report back to you the next time I get back to the bedroom," he said.

"Skip it," she said. "Lost interest," she said, "the instant I asked," she said.

"What?" he said. He said, "What was it you asked?"

"Could we fuck on it?" she said.

He said, "Would we or could we?"

"I don't want to talk about it," she said.

"Where couldn't we fuck?" he said.

"I'm getting off the line," she said. "Don't you hear something on the line?" she said.

He said, "No."

She said, "Your hearing's going."

He said, "It's yours that is."

She said, "Let's not take a chance." She said, "Hang up." She said, "If you won't, I will."

"Oh, but of course," he said. "No end to the theories of the Agamben guy. Hey," he said, "you ever hear of Alexander Graham Bell?" he said.

She said, "I'm having a test tomorrow."

"Aren't we all?" he said.

She said, "Did you hear what I said?"

He said, "What did you say?" He said, "Didn't you say you're hanging up?"

●

He said, "What's the verdict?"

She said, "It didn't come in yet."

He said, "It'll be okay."

"Probably," she said.

"No question about it," he said. "Take it easy," he said. "Did you tell him?" he said.

She said, "Tell him what?"

"I guess you started to," he said, "and he was, you know, reading," he said.

"Thanks for checking in," she said.

"No trouble at all," he said.

She said, "It's not unlikely you think there's a prize involved."

He said, "Isn't there always?"

"Shit," she said, "that's so Jewish of you."

"A fella's got to keep trucking," he said.

She said, "You're not even living in this century," she said.

He said, "Yeah, but I'll die in it, won't I?"

She said, "Call me Thursday. Chances are I'll have heard by Thursday." She said, "I want you to be the first to hear."

"Me too," he said. He said, "The same'd go for me," he said. "Isn't it crazy?" he said. He said, "After all these years."

"After all the years," she said.

●

He said, "So?"

"All clear," she said.

"Thank God," he said.

"Yeah," she said. "Until it's otherwise," she said.

"Not to dwell on it," he said.

"Right," she said. She said, "But we dwell."

He said, "What is that?" He said, "Is that Agamben again?"

"Just common sense," she said.

"Alas," he said.

"Alas, your ass," she said.

"I'm thinking yours," he said.

"I'm old," she said.

He said, "We're always old. It's ours to live," he said.

She said, "I can't."

"You won't," he said.

"The chair," she said.

He said, "Picture it." He said, "Can you picture it?" He said, "We'd lay a sheet over it."

"Drape it over it," she said.

He said, "Drape," he said. He said, "You'd bring it and we'd drape it." He said, "Together," he said. He said, "Are you seeing it?"

"I don't know," she said.

"See it," he said.

She said, "All I'm really seeing is the telephone. All I'm really seeing is what I looked like when the call came in. All I'm really seeing is his peeking into the back of the car when I'd forget to get the sheet out of it."

He said, "But that never happened, did it?"

She said, "No, it never happened. But I was so afraid," she said. "I could never remember," she said. "I was always thinking all that night did I actually get it out of the car and get it into the washing machine."

He said, "That's what you were thinking?"

She said, "I was thinking had I or hadn't I." She said, "And then I'd get up in the middle of the night to make sure I'd run a load and gotten it into the dryer or at least stuck the sheet at the bottom out of the way under the other stuff."

"Whereas me," he said, "whereas I," he said, "I was all that night thinking Jesus, your leg, your ankle, your foot—my hand, this hand." He said, "My right hand, your left leg—knee, calf, ankle, foot."

"I was terrified," she said.

"Don't be terrified," he said.

"What if the report had come out different?" she said.

"Ah, yes, that," he said. "It's always that."

She said, "He's back. I hear him. He's back."

"I'll call," he said.

She said, "Yes—call."

•

"You okay?" he said.

"Yes, I'm fine," she said.

He said, "I'm sorry. I'm suddenly stumped," he said, "for what to say."

She said, "Look at it this way—you just," she said, "managed to say something," she said.

"Okay," he said. "It's just that I all of a sudden don't feel . . . ."

"Not another word," she said. "We'll get together soon."

He said, "You mean that?"

"On the phone," she said.

"Yes, got you," he said. "On the phone," he said.

•

"You know what I used to think?" she said.

He said, "What did you used to think?"

"A woman's work," she said.

"You mean the sheet," he said. "Well, I'll tell you what I," he said, "used to think."

"Watch it," she said. "I'm not ready for any more guff," she said. "Not from you," she said. "But go ahead and tell me what," she said.

"Fine," he said. "I'm going to tell you," he said. "How tired my arm was," he said. He said, "In the midst of all that, how tired."

"That's sweet," she said. "It's sort of endearing," she said. "It's a remembrance I'll take to bed with me tonight," she said.

"Listen," he said, "I don't think I'm so certain you even know what guff means. You know what I mean?" he said.

"I know what pain means," she said.

He said, "I'll bet you do."

She said, "Don't kid yourself, buddy boy. I know what I know."

He said, "You know what you think you know."

She said, "I'm not for an instant suggesting you hurt me." She said, "You do understand that, don't you? But there was pain," she said.

"Really?" he said. "As in pain, you mean? As in ow, you mean?"

"Believe it," she said.

"I don't," he said. "You're confusing me with him," he said. He said, "It's been so long now, you don't know which is which."

"Oh, I know," she said. "Don't be so quick to flatter yourself. You dealt out your share," she said. She said, "Body pain. Not hurt, buddy boy. Not just hurt, buddy boy," she said. "But pain, darling. Not," she said, "just a weary arm, but how about cramps in my leg?" she said.

"This is childish," he said.

"Beneath us," she said.

He said, "We had the chair beneath us."

She said, "We had the carpet, the bed."

He said, "The floor sometimes. It was lovely on the floor."

"Sometimes," she said.

"All the time," he said.

"Now," she said, "now there's no time," she said.

"There's time," he said. He said, "We could arrange it," he said.

"I'm old," she said. "I'm fed up with everything," she said. She said, "I'm fed up with myself," she said.

He said, "Outgrow it," he said.

"Heart's not in it," she said.

"Try another part," he said.

"I heard something," she said.

"You heard me pleading," he said.

"Ringing off," she said.

He said, "How Brit of you—wow."

"Goodbye," she said.

"Goodbye," he said.

•

"Naugahyde," she said.

"Hunh?" he said.

She said, "Years ago you said it was Naugahyde."

"I don't understand you," he said.

She said, "You said it, you said it."

"Said what?" he said.

"Said," she said, "that she had had it recovered in Naugahyde. Or with Naugahyde. Reupholstered in it. You said it, you said it," she said, "you did. Years ago, for God's sake." She said, "Of all the things, Jesus."

"I couldn't have," he said. "What's Naugahyde?" he said. He said, "I don't even know what Naugahyde is," he said.

"You heard me," she said.

He said, "Heard what?"

She said, "You let her, you let her."

"Let her what?" he said.

"Skip it," she said.

He said, "What are we talking about?"

"It doesn't matter," she said.

"She's downstairs," he said.

She said, "That's right." She said, "Of course she is."

"Women," he said.

"It's an old saying," she said.

"I'm not following you," he said.

"For every man," she said, but did not say the rest.

•

Afterwards, for no few times afterwards, he would seek to re-member, and she would seek to remember—each succeeding a little differently from the other—remembering when they would be given to slide all as one down off the lip of the chair, oh so shiningly slidingly, together, together, each mindful to reach back a little to drag the bedsheet down along with them down onto the floor with them, her foot, her ankle, her knee, her leg, none of it not ever for an instant not still gripped in his hand, the ecstasy of it, of their rolling over and over in this unforgettable zeal, smash-ing into the whole household together, smashing into everything everywhere together, forever rolling over and over in the whole wide world together, rolling the two of them together in the rolling feeling of love.

GRIEF—2ND PASS

It was onto her back that Barbara fell one of the times she was to fall before her falling into the earth to the depth we all of us hear about long before we're all of us dead.

She didn't scream.

Didn't call out.

It may have been by then that Barbara's voice had ceased to work and that she could not be heard even to weep, except to shut her eyes and squeeze if that's what she wanted for you to know, that she was crying despite there being no tears for her to cry for you to know she needed help, needed haste, wanted for you to hurry and do something as fast as you could, or can.

No, Barbara just lay in the murk of the room looking up into my face as down into the scalloped sky of the patterned carpeting back beneath her head there spread a corona of black blood gaining concentricity by wicking its way from fiber to fiber in the drenched wool Barbara had searched the city for so that the effect of the figured floor covering would be kept in keeping with that of the figured wall covering that hung, ragged, unashamedly showy, down from the crazed brass rod arranged high into the crosspiece formed by the wall where the wall met the ceiling above the drama of our bed.

Was that too much?

Did I cram too much together for enough of it to be read without botheration, annoyance, roil?

I'm referring your reference to the crewel-work tapestry that hung then, that still hangs now, from the intersection of wall and ceiling, a period affair that descends to down behind the sleeping pillows arranged at the summit of the master bedroom bed, its theme, the theme of the crewel work, the Tree of Life—if you will please please believe the comment uttered by the crude fruit-like imagery among the stitchery of leaves and branches, here and there the scattery impressions of perched unknowable birds.

Life.

One wants to say, and I will say it: of all things!—this remark upon a room where not at all gradually were accumulating the accrued conclusive indices of death moving in.

But worse first.

To put the truest point on it, much worse did indeed, always does, I suppose, come first. The prelude to death, making space for its rude furniture, an intruder barging in to wreck the perfected affectations of a household contrived to convince you everything in it fit and that there would be no other way that it could be confected to suit its residents.

Sorry for all the rhyme.

The objects of the place had all of them taken up unbudgeable postures where Barbara had appointed them to go, and then, there in the middle of the proverbial night, Barbara herself lay like a revision of the milieu, wedged between credenza and bed, the array of disturbed decor forever awry, the chatelaine bleeding.

Is it corona or corrola, the word, and if it is corrola, then is it spelled corolla instead? Alphonso Lingis would say that it was a halo I was seeing down below the glory of Barbara's hair, blood making its widening advance, pushing out along the wool into the figment of a circle, or of a cirque, may it not be allowably said?

Unless cirque means nothing like circle or disc or halo. These are things that can be looked up, of course, checked into, but I have neither the eyesight nor the strength and patience to try to pin down what's attributed with any exaction anymore, or is it exactitude? Besides, if I leave off the enterprise of typing on the Underwood, if I lean too far away from this adventure to re-cite events, I'll never recover the gumption to take up the effort again—yet on the other hand, if that, then that, and what then, an act of remediation lost? O lost, lost, perish the thought, but what does it matter, if this, not that, if what you don't arrive with is the Big Hegel Choc Bar or the equally desired Cartesian Taffy Twists?

This was the version of grief that greeted my mother whenever she achieved a visitation to the Hebrew Home for Aged Ladies, unless it was on her return from the Home for Aged Hebrew La-dies that I am thinking of, coming in from school and finding my mother seated on her mending chair and crying chair mending and crying because my mother's mother, Ethel, had declined to receive from her daughter Reggie any of the substitute treats that might have been fetched from any of the confectionaries to be found in the five boroughs because there was no Big Hegel Choc Bar anywhere for sale, nor, unless it is or, the option of a bag of Cartesian Taffy Twists that Ethel would, according to Reggie, sometimes demand her daughters be sent to scour the city for.

This is a sampling of the calamities abroad in the sea of fam-ily hygiene, as if you already had not—Jesus, Jesus!—known, or won't. Uh-oh, left out the part where the child of the marriage hears the commotion and comes rushing into the bedroom to say, "What have you done to my mother? Get away from my mother, you bastard! Are you crazy, stop looking at my mother and go do something! It's blood and she's bleeding, you sonofabitch—get the fuck out of here, go!"

Mmm, another datum left unobserved—the Cratchit-like apparatus I've been sitting on, which Barb picked out for me for when I work on the Underwood at this table, just to tell you it's been hell on the back, that—no, the word I want, it's not that one, it's something truer—it's stool, it's stool. Ah, nearly forgot: the dream I never stop getting, or is it having?—the boy there, me there, I'm all *oh, good, good, now tighter, tighter, tight*. Oh boy, nothing but *tighter, tighter, tight*. It's so wonderful. It's all I have. Not much, but who can beat it for terrific? Listen, as the gospels teach, if you're willing to play along with fiddle-faddle like that—enough is enough. Is it not enough? In Hebe, I mean, isn't there in the song "Dayenu," it's a thing like that, isn't there? I mean, isn't there like a resignation in it which keeps dumdee-dumming like that? Not that there's any selection, mmm?

Hey, didn't it slip what's left of my mind to remember to tell you Reg was always telling me Gramma was always dispatching the girls to go get the heck out there and go scavenge her up a couple of handfuls of these mini bags (baglettes, she said baglettes, did she?) of these Schopenhauer Crusted Chips all the other luckier, better-beloved ladies were always raving over, were so fabled all over everywhere for a nickel a pop up there on some perfectly heimische corner up in the Bronx?

Yeah, I did, I did.

Darn it—darn!

Lord God, doesn't it sometimes seem all a child does is forget and forget?

•

el au: Replace "Underwood" with "Smith-Corona" *passim?*

au/e: Thanx. Tempting, but retain "Underwood" per DeLillo ref anon.

au/e: ¶ **19**, 1st sentence, make "stool" "widget."

au/e: Last ¶, penultimate line, skip it.

TALE OF A HORSE

I suppose the moment is more or less upon me for me to sit myself down here and try to tell you a well-rounded thing about Kenneth Elton Kesey, seeing as how there's hardly been an adequation of death, this of his son Jed and of himself, the boy Jed first, this by vehicular means, thereafter the father Ken, kidney or kidneys, time, with its uncountable opportunities betwixt the two occurrences, making room enough for the father to write, in dedication to, or for, the dead child, this, the following:

To Jed, across the river and riding point.

Unless it was *For Jed* and not *To Jed* that Kesey actually wrote. And, not impossibly, he wrote no *and*.

Me, I can't say which or what, can I? Don't have the book to refer to. It was, of course, neither *One Flew Over the Cuckoo's Nest* nor *Sometimes a Great Notion* that the dedication to the dead child appeared in. All I can offer you by way of informing you of further information is opinion: to wit, that it was a lesser book Kesey dedicated to his dead son, writers often writing lesser books after their having written greater books and then, for reasons of most writers being hounded by being human, writers of such a temperament not quitting while they're ahead. Or to put the point less complainingly, if you've got greater, you needs must have not greater, or, in a word, lesser. But perhaps Kesey had no idea he was so far ahead.

Of the game, as the saying goes.

Is there any telling what somebody knows about what's being done relative to what's been done? The worth of it, I mean—of this compared with that. What I do most emphatically know, however, is that I trembled when I read, or is it came upon, that dedication to the dead Jed and, as a result, sensed myself in readiness for tears.

But I didn't cry.

I don't, as a rule, cry.

Oh damn, but just realized there was a time when I did cry, old enough to have put a stop to it but didn't, just sobbed and sobbed, this in the company of one of mine.

Children, that is.

Of all things!

Like Kesey, I have had kids in both regimes.

Girls and boys.

Men and women.

I will not name Kesey's other children for fear of my poking into their privacy and thus conniving with the avidity of a practitioner patrolling the codings of the civil law, which I am guessing may be subject to state-to-state, or is it state-by-state, readings?

Who knows?

I am too old to know anymore much of what might be known. I do, howsoever, know that I have indeed gone and named my children in scribblage of my own.

You think they'll sue?

It's not impossible, is it?

When it comes to the actions of daughters and sons and of mothers and fathers, what, under the most promising of torrents, given the lovingest of intentions, can confidently be foretold never to come scandalously, invidiously, insidiously to pass?

When Kesey said what he said about the dead Jed, Kesey's love and pride and goodwill endowed, to my mind, every scintilla of what the man said with the untellable beauty that can only be revealed between a giver of life and a recipient of same. Ah, but don't we all of us know of instances aplenty when neither party can bear, abide, embrace the attention of the other?

Lucky Ken, lucky Jed—that the luck we all of us want outlasted the lucklessness we all of us get.

To Jed—across the river riding point.

Or was it *For Jed, across the river and riding point?*

It may have been *For*—and so on and so forth.

The permutations, especially when a great writer is paying great attention, won't they try a lesser writer's patience in a whip-stitch?

Such a writer might lean on a particular word overmuch.

Such as the word *point*.

Such a writer might say *This book is for Jed, who died.* Such a writer might write dedication after dedication, and then, in the end, abandon the creation of a surtext, that writer's having come to decide the feeling was not equal to the occasion of producing a headnote memorializing the deceased child, or vice versa.

I remember I trembled and very nearly cried.

I remember thinking Kesey is a terrific father whose heart is terrifically broken.

I remember thinking the majesty of it, the majesty!

I remember feeling oh God, Gordon, you don't have it in you, do you?

I remember there was more than a touch of envy in my feeling.

When the town authorities supervening over Palo Alto's infamous Perry Lane had chased away the tenants of the shacks thereon, Kesey, among them, picked up his family and work-in-progress and acquired, in La Honda, an outpost in the faraway foothills, a sprawling setup with acreage to spare. Up the way from the house, up toward a clearing that Jed, unless it was not Jed but another of Kesey's children, had dubbed Barking Bug Meadow, and it was in this clearing, in Barking Bug Meadow, we often foregathered to tell tales, gaze at the crown of a certain very tall tree that stood very nearby, hum in the lulls, doze in the lulls, smoke most of the time, disagree all of the time.

There was a time when we had been doing all of the foregoing, when whereupon (otiose but fun) doing just that, Kesey got to his feet, went hustling down to the house, came hurtling back with a spade and a kid's hollow toy, the tin of which was wrought to resemble a horse with the likeness of the species thereof printed, gaily, on it, this side, that side, a hollow tin horse, a toy, a plaything that may have been Jed's, the family's youngest.

Well, I'm not just guessing: I'm arranging the cards.

Kesey crushed the toy in his hand, stomped on it, and at the base of that tree I remarked, the very tall one I mentioned, while I and my children and Ken's children and his missus all stood by and watched, Kesey took the spade and dug a hole and dropped in the squashed metal, the hooves having lost their pertinence in the mangle. Then the man took paper from my oldest's homework and, with the stub of a thick red crayon that Kesey got from his pocket, he wrote:

Whacha lookin' down in here for, Daisy-Mae?

Laid the paper over the destroyment, a word I'm asking to slip in and just, permissionless, did.

Kicked over it the soil he'd spaded out.

Buried the whole affair.

Toy and message.

Tamped it down with his boot.

Tamped it down very carefully, very firmly—say emphatically, say hard.

I and mine went back down the hill and drove back home. I don't think any of us said word one about the toy horse in ruin or about the writing the writer had written on the loose-leaf paper. I thought, sure, he's just itching for somebody to come along as far in the future as you and I are right this instant now, dig around the tree as people will, uncover the wrecked plaything, the digger taken, at long last, in.

Whoa!

Well, she had been, hadn't she?

Daisy-Mae, that is.

Me, I was much impressed with the apostrophe. Oh, but of course an apostrophe can just as much refer to the effect of address too, can't it? Also, me, I made certain the hyphen was entered when I first told this tale—yet, in all fairness, I was tested on the point only once before. I mean, I say, "Hey, when the man wrote the name Daisy-Mae, had he not shown himself capable of punctuality to a fault, yes or no?"

Jed was a college boy when the van he was riding in with the rest of the wrestling team was making its way back from a meet and went off the highway, and kept on going, down a ravine.

You say it was a prophecy that greeted Jed there at the conclusion of that fall?

I say you may be on to something, Daisie May.

I say when it comes to writing, watch your step.

On the other hand, I also say never you mind, there's just too much for you to forfend against when you scribble, unless scribble's a dismissably playful word, one deficient in taunting the peril coiled most gainfully in the telling of the simplest, most harmless tale.

You know.

So here we are, agawp and agog with the truth. But, hey, what diddle can't be tied to what fiddle, providing the amenable faculty of time is, as it ever agreeably insists, on the job?

Agreeably?

Wrong word, wrong word—but only the devil's dictionary lists the right one. And as for *punctuality* back there, I was jumpy and in a hurry, so say I said "a punctum" and we'll call it square.

VICISSITUDES OF PLOT

She said, "Take them if you want them."

She had opened the drawer, and said, "Take some if you want."

She drew the drawer open and said, "If you want some, take some."

The drawer was almost all of the way open.

She said, "Are you getting a load of this?"

Was she going to pull it out too far?

She said, "Go ahead, take."

I said, "I never saw so many at once."

She said, "It was his nature to stock up on things."

I said, "Mine too."

She said, "Staples. He always stocked staples."

I said, "Me too. Lots of stuff. But not these. Jeez, no."

She said, "Expense wasn't a thing with him."

I said, "It is with me."

She said, "Don't be shy. Take what you want."

I bet it was the kind of drawer you can't pull out too far.

She said, "Talk about hoarding, I could show you something."

I said, "Me, it's canned tuna, canned corn, instant coffee."

She said, "We only used fresh."

I said, "Yeah—brewed, right—that's great."

She jounced the drawer. She said, "Go ahead, take."

I said, "Yeah, and how about chopsticks, straws, cotton napkins?"

She gave the drawer a jiggle. She said, "Please. Take."

I said, "And how about paper napkins?"

She said, "Paper napkins? That's wacky—paper."

I said, "I know, I know."

Tell you the truth, I was trying to get a bead on how many.

Stalling, I said, "Tupperware, natch."

She said, "Well, who doesn't do that?"

I said, "Sweet'N Low, Splenda."

She said, "What's that other one? There's another one."

Truth to tell, I was eyeing the drawer.

I said, "Yeah, a third one, there's a third, you're right."

She said, "He wouldn't touch the stuff. Sugar or nothing."

I said, "The man was a purist, you can sure see that."

She pushed the drawer back in a little.

I said, "Not me. I'm happy to make do with whatever."

She said, "I like that." She said, "A regular guy, good."

I said, "I get by."

She said, "Hey, I'll bet you do."

It looked to me like there were all you ever would need in there.

She said, "You want to see some tennis balls?"

I said, "Thanks, but no, it's not my game."

She said, "Untouched. Brand-new. Vacuum-packed."

I said, "Shit, no. Really?"

Wilkerson Swords! The fucking things were Wilkersons!

She said, "Like this greeny color. Of the moment, you know?"

I said, "I think it's an E-word probably."

She said, "What?

I said, "The third one."

She said, "Third?"

I said, "Never mind."

She said, "How do you say that—one or two words?"

"Say what?" I said.

She said, "Oh, you mean Equal, Equal!—right?"

I said, "Didn't you say you never used that stuff?"

"Him," she said. She said, "Me, I'm no stickler for nothing."

I figured there were enough to last me to the last shave.

She said, "He was the purist." She said, "Me, it's all context."

Wilkerson or Wilkinson?

She said, "Blue."

I said, "Hunh?"

She said, "Equal. The packaging, it's the blue one."

Too far away to tell, but Brit ones for sure. Imported. Shit, yeah.

She said, "Wait here and I'll show you."

I said, "It's okay."

She said, "No, really—I'll prove it to you. Blue."

I said, "Skip it. It doesn't matter."

Was she going to shut the drawer? Did she mean the sweetener or the tennis balls?

I said, "Let me see something."

She said, "Huh?"

I said, "Let me get a better look."

She said, "I said I'll go show you."

She started up.

I said, "No, please—don't go, don't."

She settled back down. She said, "Easy, baby, take it easy."

I said, "It's fine, we're fine."

"We've got all the time in the world," she said.

I said, "Fat chance. Nobody does."

She said, "Oh, you. Don't be so grumpy," she said.

"Here today, gone tomorrow," I said.

"I go for the here today," she said.

"Who doesn't?" I said. "What else is there?" I said.

"Well," she said, "one thing you can say is he's not."

"From the look of it," I said, "he did all right," I said.

She said, "You mean these?" She gave the drawer a bounce.

I said, "Top of the line, they look like."

She said, "Yeah—nothing cut-rate for him, count on it."

I said, "There's a ton of them here, man oh man."

"Yeah," she said. She said, "The guy took his pick."

I said, "Those tennis balls must be pips, you know?"

She said, "You want me to go check the brand?"

I said, "No, no—just stay—stay."

She said, "Listen, the fella had taste."

"Believe me," I said, "who can't see that?"

She said, "Talk about treating yourself to the best."

I said, "A connoisseur like."

She said, "You can say that again."

"Hey, lady," I said, "if I could I would."

"Oh, a comedian," she said. "I like that," she said.

I took a chance, and said, "Among other things, sure."

She said, "Who doesn't like a guy who knows how?"

I said, "Cotton napkins, honey. Some of them even linen."

She said, "Like you swiped them, am I right?"

I said, "Sometimes what's the choice?"

"A man who takes," she said.

"I have my moments," I said.

I touched her fingertips where they were touching the drawer.

"Go ahead," she said.

I said, "The blades?"

"They're every one of them yours if you want," she said.

I could see that. Terrific. They were mine, by God.

I said, "Nowadays, wherever you go, they're all synthetic."

"Tell me about it," she said.

I said, "Like a blend or something."

She said, "I've been around. I know what's going on."

I said, "Not that a blend doesn't get the job done."

She said, "But all-cotton, all-cotton feels nice. And linen."

I said, "That's what it's about—like how it feels, you know?"

Together we pulled the drawer out enough for me to see better.

She said, "Like it's not like he's ever going to be using them, right?"

I said, "No, not even one of them once," I said.

She said, "Take them all."

I said, "Madam, these are Wilkinsons. Damn."

She said, "Whatever."

I said, "I'll need a bag or something."

"Don't worry," she said.

I was going to try to pull the drawer all the way out.

She said, "You want we should dump them on the floor right here?"

I said, "Would that be okay?"

She said, "It's not like we need anything to put it in."

She mean it or them? I say she was maybe referring to about how old she was.

But I was thinking, Gordo, keep this to a line apiece at a time.

Which it worked out I was doing and nearly did until I couldn't because I didn't have the props for it.

DOES THIS MEAN ANYTHUGNG?

Do you think it means anything? Foretells anything? Forbodes? That laat word, is it spelt right? Would it be better spelt, rightly spelt, if it were spelt thus: forebodes? Now that I see the spelling spelt thus, forebodes, it does not look right to me. Oh, pity, just got a look back, saw 'laat'. Meant to say last. XDorry. You thin this means anything? I mean fea,lly means it. Ohm God, now see spelt one, two, gtheee words wrong. No, now two more. Thagt's three plus two. Spelt five wirds wrong. Now see wo more. No, three. Dol that's five plus three. Gves eight. Uhp-oh, looking back. There's wo forf two, Dol for so, Gves for Gives. Thfee more. That's eleven. Plus Thfee for Three. Oh, skipped Uhp. Uhp was supposed to be Uh. That's thurteen. Thazt's fourteen. Thagt's fiftee. That's sixteen. Very foreboding. Bodes badly. Bodes not well. Is it a A foretelling I am beng told? It doesn;t look good. Oh, gthat's seventeen. And ghat's for that, that's eighteen lor orobaakh nineteen. Plus shat's for that's agaub. No, nineteen, twenty. Do yoiu thuib this means anythung? D yurt thunk it's the keeys or me? It may be it mneans the oewriter'w keys are too close tigethet the way thewy're arranged on te thypewiter'skeyboard. Not eniugh room fr mh fingertips to touch te keys cledanly. Or des it means mhy fingertips are undergi-ing a chaned. Growng largwer. bgger Thckere. Becoming hideus.

Asfingertips go. If that's the ase, then it means my body is changing. It cannbot be that my vsy isa changng fr the better. Can it? I just heard somethung below me hit the celig of the aoartment beneath mine. ZA bhammer? It woulkd alpoeafs a workman is hammering on the ceiling of the apartment beneath mine. O has it hapened that beneath is no longer te word in e is meant to choose to express such an ibsrvratiin. ??? Perahsos it'sd underneath o below. There it goes agaiun / Or went agaun. Yes, did I nkit receiv e a legtgefr fro m tnhr persl who new,hy bught that apartment that t woujlkd be undergling a renoi aton for the next en mk tbs? K djd I did. o this isd the edence of the dependabikitgy of tha lettefr. The ,legter said that if tere is any damage caused my apartment, the premises, tghe owner if the apartment below, the new owner ofd the apartment below, wulkd indeminify me agauanst all kosses suffered by myb walls floors and so on. Tha's right. Persons of authority czmse in. Sekeks s ago. Came wth camewrs. Persons repfresentingb the new owner and persons presumaby represednting me. That staff here, jperintendent, assistangt sulintendent, Tooik pictures lof everythung. EDne en of te insides f cosets To estabeisg the status of the pre/renvwtion state of things. In my apatt,ment. There t gies agaun, More hammmerfgn. Must be hammeringon fhe ceiling down tghere fr I xcan feel it on my feet uo here. The eloor is reasing reacting. Trembl,ing. Does tbis means anythunbg. Is a ytbung foretolkd by thius. I'mgoign yki go lok the word forfblde. up I a, going t ceck to see how it's selt. Lisen, hw I ba ve lokked it up and sen seen , I wn ;t be ckming back. This is tg fre this. This is it fr thnbg. Can ;t keep cubtng. Xloe„n hg XS Se,k, Spe„king. Canng keep the ckut cujn count sarfiught. Gkos-bye. Sorrgreu fr wastbg yojur tne. Xkrrg Zkrrgr. Am so ashamedcx. Glold nrist.igt means smetghing, all rgnt! I know that every tung nmeanns sinethung but tid fealy means ut!

IN SEPTEMBER

There was a time when nothing was so important to me as growing up old enough for me to get money enough for me to get a pair of penny loafers. Imagine it. Can you imagine it, that there was a time in your life when there was nothing as important to you as this thing, and if it were not this thing, then it was that thing?

There were times in my life when it was like that.

The leaves of brown
come tumbling down
September
in September
in the rain.

My son Ethan was born in November. My son Atticus was born in September. There was a time in my life when nothing was so important to me as the births of these sons. Unless it was that there was a time in my life when the most important thing to me in my life was my daughters, when I would take them out of doors with me to go outside with me to garden in the yard with me, Jennifer, born in October, Rebecca, born in December.

The leaves of brown
come tumbling down
September
in September
in the rain.

Where we all of us dwelled together when we all of us dwelled together, it was in a cottage, it was in a bungalow, it was in a little low-roofed house on Concord Way, the number of it cised into the little gabled door like this—NO. 7 1 1—do you see, did you see?—a detail which we would all of us take care to pronounce seven eleven for the good fortune in it. Oh, the good fortune we all of us had in that little low-roofed house, a playground one street, no, two streets away, in that direction over there, whereas going the other way was the way you would go to deliver a child to the kindergarten, and thereafter to collect the child and to conduct it—ah, to accompany it—over the course of the little walk homeward.

Home.

Schoolward was the way you went if you had a motorcar and were in need of fuel for it when you were not far away from Concord Way—the Gulf Oil Station could be found the schoolward way, unless it was the Shell Oil Station that could be found when one were going that way—but we did not have a motorcar back in the long-ago day I am telling you about, nor a mother in the little low-roofed house neither.

If it comes to that, and of course it does indeed come to that.

The leaves of brown
come tumbling down
September

in September
in the rain.

The time I am telling you about was too long ago for me to regain details such as certain details the specifics of whose particularity would hardly have mattered to us if I had selected the right details in the first place.

We had no motorcar.

We liked to say it that way—not automobile but motorcar.

We liked to say bungalow, say cottage, say seven eleven on Concord Way.

The leaves of brown
come tumbling down
September
in September
in the rain.

It was a very little house. The doors did not have locks on them. Indeed, no door inside of nor into the little house did. You could not lock any of the doors that had anything to do with the little house. But I do not think locklessness ever made any of the children afraid.

Or, anyhow, very afraid.

I think we may have thought the two big trees that swung over the house made us safe inside.

Well, I told the children they did—beech, ash, eucalyptus—a pair of very big trees probably akin to something like one of those which I just named.

Jennifer.

Rebecca.

Ethan.

Atticus.

The leaves of brown
come tumbling down
September
in September
in the rain.

I must admit that, insofar as I was concerned, the little house conferred an exalted status on those who lived in it. This feeling I sought to aggrandize with drawings I would encourage be undertaken by persons stopping by, if claims of artistry had been made, for back in those accomplished days it was not at all uncommon for a talent in visualizing to be stated, and when it rather often was, one of us would hurry to bring out drawing paper and very sharpened pencils and the drawing pen we kept at the ready for the uses of historiographing our cornering of beauty—a gift, it was, a house gift, it was, a housewarming expression of community proffered, as the practice had been back in those gullible days.

Who knows?

It may still have it that way.

One might be brought a bit of something if someone happened by, or had even made it a point to contrive a visit.

Come see us.

That sort of thing.

You know what I mean.

Probable mothers not impossibly did.

Skip it.

Who really remembers?

What I remember is how, just to the side of me, oh how strict was the manner of the child who stood standing in a version of orthodox attention, every stitch of the body devoted to the bearing up of a tray of baffled foundlings arraigned for me to scoop each one free from where it sat waiting in furious aspiration.

Everything now is now so long ago.

You must know what I mean.

Oh, flat, flat—I think the nurseryman called such a tray a flat.

The leaves of brown
come tumbling down
September
in September
in the rain.

We mainly spent what money we could manage honoring the little house with plantings and with primpings to the appearance it would cut when the neighbors might lean over to favor us with a look, when passersby would be willing to pretend to inspect our exception, especially when we ourselves stood beholding the place in the mood prescribed for a late-afternoon swoon in a Sunday species of light.

We were all of us mad for the little funny-roofed house.

It bestowed, bespoke, betokened grandeur on a deftly limited deliriously precious kind of scale.

You could propose it to yourself—I did, I never didn't!—in a picture book, in a storybook, in a make-believe era in a make-believe world—ours, all ours, resolutely, stoically, defiantly, the Lish house, little and darling, little and brave.

Do you see it?

Exquisite.

The plantings.
Do you see us?
A family.
More or less.
Okay, here we go again.

The leaves of brown
come tumbling down
September
in September
in the rain.

Making our way just beyond the village laundromat onward
to the village nursery to fetch home a tray of something plantable
where there was no mother to pitch in, no mother to lend a hand,
no mother to assist, no chatelaine to come with a watering can, or
do I just say any or all of this for want of feelings to correspond
with the word watering, the word assist, the word lend?

Yes, that's what I think it was which the nurseryman would
call it, counseling us by dint of his silence for us to so call the
tray too, flat, a flat, this bounded span of possibles—sproutlings,
seedlings, appliqués of abidings that would twist your heart with
yearning, all the weekend long, of that glorious implication that
enclosed us with its ecstasies, spending what we could scrape together for us to spend among the discounted choices, hastening
back across the railroad tracks with a child or two or three or four
for fear the striplings in their fabulous containment would perish
in the morning chill before, one by one, each prospect could be
laid beneath a quilting of soil so cozy so loamy that . . .

I'm so sorry.
This is so very tiring for me.

So cozy so loamy that what—or is it so what?

I don't know how best I might have filled in something wordful enough back there for it to duly do the ding back there.

Jennifer, then Rebecca—Ethan, then Atticus.

The leaves of brown
come tumbling down
September
in September
in the rain.

The idea was to develop the grounds, make sallyings forth over the railroad tracks to the village nursery where whatever you took home with you turned out for it to always have been perfect, just right—incredibly benevolently tastefully on sale.

"Here, Mr. Lish, you can have what's in this flat for a dollar if you get the box back to us before the close of business tomorrow."

Those quotation marks, you needn't be told they're excusably fraudulent.

Oh, how solemn stood the child who stood.

All those ess words—solemn, studious, sober, stern.

Sullen?

Severe?

No, my friend, no!—yet I do indeed concede these were serious children who wished only to take part, to be of service, to stand gardening with Daddy while Daddy gardened, who stood each of them with such solemnity, with such gravity, with such— well, they were poised children, forever poised as little children go, a little austere possibly, not impossibly a little wearied, holding out a chuggyjam tray trembling with it steadied for Daddy, Daddy crouched at his country labors, householder using the big kitchen spoon to get out the next numinous thing to go in and commence its goddamn growing, goddamn it to goddamn hell.

You know what I mean.

You can see what I mean.

The leaves of brown
come tumbling down
September
in September
in the rain.

Get the tender thing scooped gently out and settled down into the place in the earthy loam that had been opened for it to glow in, beaming back its scrumptious promise of durability at us, its accordance with belonging, with its being enfolded, its brazen consent to the pledge of our scheme.

Or say I said loamy earth.

The father knelt, the big kitchen spoon both blackened and shining, the child standing alongside, whichever child, stern aspect, stolid affect, the house-proud family bent to its superlative enchantment—sort of superlatively smitten.

The child, a child, solidly standing.

Holding the burden of our worth aloft.

The rest is figurative.

Even that much of it, every fraction of it, it's already debased by its being prose.

What matter?

Is there harm in it?

Nobody loses an eye when all it is is just an old man conniving with sentences whilst asquat on his tuffet at an old man's table.

Or vice versa.

The leaves of brown
come tumbling down
September
in September
in the rain.

But how about this?

That dyad of bushy leviathans swooping—swooped!—down onto the wig-a-poo kick-a-poo hugga-mugga cottage, bungalow, property, our property, stance—how about just that right there!

My children.

This gatherment.

Everything grew in it.

Anything grew in it.

The loam alone, as folly might prompt one to say, and I just said it.

It was so wonderful to dig with the big kitchen spoon down into the helpmeet of it, that pillowy ooey reciprocity the nursery-man told us could not be other than the loam of Concord Way.

The terrific good fortune of it.

Seven eleven Concord Way.

Like this—NO. 7 1 1 scored into the arch of the cookie-house door.

Jen.

Bec.

Eth.

Att.

Very serious, very solemn—what word did I choose?

Did I say stern?

I laid things into the earth there.

All of it flourishing, success a certainty, that lucky address.

Assurances spreading from thing to thing, flower, shrub, hedge—an earnest privet encircling the whole unscrupulous affair, the mossy brick curdling of a broken chimney gamely battling the colossal elms overhead, or oaks or stringbarks or whatever the what-have-you they were, for I do not know what in God's name those horrors were—for room for all of it to breathe, get its measure of breath, let us all of us agree to say it, for eminence, for dignity, for air?

The leaves of brown
come tumbling down
September
in September
in the rain.

Lovely.

Ever lovelier.

It was like words in a song a fairy tale made.

Daddy's little helper.

Whichever child.

Arms outstretched.

The tray, the flat, leafless biddies, row on row, aching for the impression of maternity.

Arms stretched out all of the way out.

Saturday.

Sunday.

Such greenery.

The home we were almost all of us in.

In-dwelling in.

The hyphen, that hyphen, was it unnecessary?

Just mentionably excessive just mentioning it?
The very word—hapless, shameless, a swindler's fucking snare.

The leaves of brown
come tumbling down
September
in September
in the rain.

The new people there, rumor of abuses reached us over the years.

Accusations, evidence of different sensitivities.

I mean the people who came to occupy the place did—philistines, barbarians, crass influxion of a scandal and a half.

Succulents, ocotillo, acacia, sotol, not improbably juniper pine, even palmilla and grama and cholla and sage.

Oh, and carrizo cane.

Or so we heard—and may have thereafter ornamented the defamation—the rudeness of it, the offense in it, georgics itself scorned, repudiated, sent thither on zigzags of impious confusionary strains.

I remember the children seemed not to remember the old habitation.

How green it was—all those words—lush, voluptuous, verdant, verdance, unless it's spelled verdence and is not even a word as such, even disruptively not all that G R E E E E N to begin with.

Or is it correct to say had been—as to how green it all of it was, it being, that is, NO. 7 1 1 Concord Way.

The leaves of brown
come tumbling down

September
in September
in the rain.

Well, they are, of course, all of them gone from me now.

Of course.

I, for my part, think of them not often and, when I seldom do, I must tell you that I sense myself entered by a dispensation of superb unfamiliarity, desert flora in forlorn profile on an otherwise empty plain, nothing much to be encountered there, nought to tarry for for a further rapturous look at it, no reason to pause respectful of surprise.

Isn't exhausted the word?

Let me tell you this, though.

It's strange.

It is rather as if passages—no, colorful tailings—that I have read in books, wherein features of the relentless firmament were being treated, have somehow usurped the presences of everything else to do with this bounty I have been speaking of, these children, this offspring, and that my mind, that a father's mind, has in flying buttress of his benison only what writers of a scrappy knowhowy spleen have written—a vicious disposition of scrub, of nopal, of whitehorn, of catclaw, of switchback and willow bracken, and of something someone matchlessly able has memorialized as the high chaparral.

Were I younger, stronger, spryer, actually interested to any actionable degree, or is it extent, I'd get myself up and see if I could get that last one looked up—inasmuch as up on a dictionary stand there is a big dictionary standing very near to almost alongside me, and I only have to reach, take up the magnifying glass, shove around the pages in the way, spot the entry—chaparral, high chaparral, the high chaparral, and then maybe confirm the spelling of the word silhouette.

The leaves of brown
come tumbling down
September
in September
in the rain.

The dictionary.

A house gift, as it were, from—oh, no question about it—from one of the dead mothers, I reckon it must be, or to have been, who meant, in all loving grace, to improve the household with the reference's utility, abetting the tenants left behind by her absence.

Landsakes, did you ever!

Let me tell you—if I ever again have it in me again to look anything up again, it had better be the identifying of whoever it was who thought up the words of those haintings hauntings sonorities we have been listening to. I mean, you know—those ones, these ones, the ones coming, the constituent blue authorities of our old true refrain.

The leaves of brown
come tumbling down
September
in September
in the rain.

PHYSIS VERSUS NOMOS

So I says to the window-shade man, I says to him you see this window shade, this window shade's no good, this window shade is beat to shit, this window shade has been in my window since who knows when, I need a new window shade, how about a new window shade, you got another window shade for me just like this one, and so the window-shade man takes the window shade from me and the window-shade man, he says to me just like this one, just like this one, there can be no window shade just like this one, even this one cannot be just like this one when you said to me just like this one since this one is now not a window shade in your hands, this one is now a window shade in my hands, whereupon I says to the window-shade man yeah but barring all that, but barring all that, let's get down to cases, cases, says the window-shade man, you want cases, says the window-shade man, here's cases for you just to begin with, says the window-shade man, as in see this grommet you got here in this window shade, what we do here is we don't do a thing like this grommet you got here, you want a grommet, you don't come here, you want a grommet in it as far as a window shade, you go down the block you get a grommet in it as far as a window shade, down the block they do it for you with a grommet in it for you as far as a window shade for you, here we do it with you screw in this thing here like a button here and then the pull itself, you take the loop like this and it goes around and winds around it like it's like a button you're winding the loop of the pull around, but grommet forget about it, grommet you're spinning your wheels, you have to have a grommet in it, then we are not the window-shade people for you and your people, you have to have a grommet in it, the window-shade people for you, these are the window-shade people down the block or up the block depending on which direction, that's where they do a grommet, that's where you get a grommet, this place we don't do a grommet, this place you can't get a grommet, us what we do here is you get home and you screw in this screw-in thing which is like a button we give you at the bottom in the stick on this side, on that side, whichever side you want and then the pull, all you do is you take the loop and go wind it any way you want to wind, the wind is up to you the way you decide you want to wind it, but a grommet, not a grommet, you want a grommet, you go to the other people, they can do a grommet for you if a grommet is what you want, but so are we doing business with you or are we facing an impasse with you as far as the stipulation with the grommet with you, and so I says to the window-shade man, I says to him the only thing different if I go ahead and get the window shade with you people and not with the other people is with you people the grommet, it's just the grommet, or is what you're telling me is there are other things which you are going to tell me which are also in the nature of things which are going to be different as far as the window shade we're getting rid of, whereupon the man says to me, whereupon the window-shade man says to me brackets, let's talk brackets, let's review what at your residence the situation is as far as brackets, which way are you set up in your residence as far as your brackets, and so I says to the window-shade man brackets, you mean when you say brackets you mean these like bracket things which they go up there where you screw them into the wall with like these anchors or something, plugs, up into the insides up at the top of the window and you get up and you hang the window shade from them, like these two little things which one of them goes on one side and the other one goes on the other side, those things like brackets are what you mean when you say to me brackets, and so the window-shade man says to me sided, they're sided, they're like one side is for one side and the other side is for the other side on the other side, so the question which I am asking you is which way do you want for us to set you up with the window shade we're making for you as far as replacing the old window shade with regard to the question of conforming to the old brackets, or is it in your thinking at this stage of the game what you want for your agenda to look like is you take out the old ones which went with this window shade here and get us to give you new ones so you can start over fresh from the beginning with new ones, in which case don't forget we also have to charge you for new plugs as far as anchoring it, and so I says to the window-shade man, I say to him look, it should only all I know is roll up so it's rolling up on the outside and not up on the inside and so it's facing out on the side facing into the window, this cuff down here at the bottom where it turns around and makes the opening where the stick is, or goes through.

"Oh," he says.

"What's the matter?" I say.

The window-shade man says to me, "Go home and look it over and get your agenda straight before you come in here with things like this for me when you are obviously so obviously ill-prepared to go ahead and do business with me as your preferred window-shade tradesperson in the neighborhood." The window-shade man says to me, "This is not a criticism. Don't take this as a criticism. It is not my policy here to stand here and offer criticism." The window-shade man says to me, "I am giving guidance. I am giving counsel. Do not take it as a rebuff. Do not take it as a reproof. First go see what's your setup as far as the specifics so you can come in here unencumbered and act freely like a human being unfettered by the conditions."

So I says to the window-shade man, "Look, believe me, I am here on your premises in good faith and am ready and able to do business with you with a clear conscience as a fully endowed citizen in complete possession of his wits as well as his teleology."

"Yeah," the window-shade man says to me, "but I'm not arguing, it's not an argument, no one here is standing here endeavoring to take issue with you as far as an argument, but the brackets," the window-shade man says to me, "your qualification with the brackets is they go this way or they go that way, which is not for one minute to say they can't go up and get screwed in either way which you want them to, but once they're in on whichever side which you screw each one of them in on, everything devolves from that fact and therefore develops the repercussion of which way the window shade rolls, does the window shade roll in or does the window shade roll out. So you understand what I'm saying?" the window-shade man says. "Devolves or debouches."

"How could I not understand what you're saying?" I says. "I understand what you're saying," I says. "But I'm just saying myself," I says.

"Stay with me with this," says the window-shade man. "You mention cuff. I heard you mention cuff. Okay, cuff. Talk to me, talk to me—you want the cuff you can see from the inside or you can't—which or which?"

"Right," I says, "right." I says to the window-shade man, I says to him, "This is the question," I says, "and the answer to the question is I don't know if I can answer this question with an un-cluttered mind."

"Well, it's your brackets," the window-shade man says. "It all goes back to your brackets," the window-shade man says. "We're getting nowhere with this until we get a better grip on your past setup as far as brackets," the window-shade man says. "But," the window-shade man says, "this is where your age-old question as far as volition comes in. Plus, you know, plus ataraxy."

"You mean at home," I says.

"Check," the window-shade man says. "So what you do is you turn around and you go home and you get home and you look up there at the top of the window and you see what your situation shapes up like on a current basis as far as shall I say the siddedness of your brackets and then you turn around and you come back here to me here and you talk to me and the two of us will do business or not do business, but first we got to know what we are talking about as far as what is in the wall as of now and is it to continue on in it on the current basis or be reversed."

I says, "You want me to go home and look."

He says, "That's it—you go home and you look."

I says, "Right, right, but like what am I looking at?"

"Where you stand with the brackets," says the window-shade man. "What your setup is as far as the brackets," the window-shade man says. "What's what as far as the current siddedness when you get up on a stool and you inspect each respective bracket con-stituting the totality of your brackets non-dereistically."

"And that's it?"

"Providing we don't come to an aporia as far as the cuff and so forth," he says.

"But no grommet is what you're telling me no matter what, an affection for dereism notwithstanding."

"No matter what, you get no grommet for the pull, not here. What you get here for the pull is you get this screw-in thing we give you instead. See? Like a button. It's like a button with this like screw-in thing it's got on it sticking out going one way. Whereas what you already got yourself here on this one, it's a grommet. See this? This is a grommet. But me, when you do business here in this place with us as your window-shade people, it's exclusively this button treatment which I give you—lucid yes or lucid no?"

"Definitely, definitely," I says to him. "But so I should like go home, you're saying to me," I says to the window-shade man.

"Go home," the window-shade man says to me.

"See what the setup is."

"The situation," the window-shade man says to me.

"Check it out," I says.

"Check out the brackets," the window-shade man says to me. "Then you come back here and we get down to cases with a grasp of what the score is. Or you go up the block. Because you can always, you know, go up the block. There is always the freedom of you go up the block. Because with some people it's grommet and the question of the cuff is secondary or even absent."

"It's not a factor with me, I don't think."

"The grommet's not."

"The way I feel about it now at this stage of the game, the grommet is a non-issue."

"I know this," the window-shade man says. "I appreciate this," the window-shade man says. "I have every confidence," the window-shade man says.

"I can go with the screw-in," I says to him.

"The button," he says.

"I can definitely go with it," I say.

"Go home," says the window-shade man. "Get up on a stool. Take a look. See what your situation is. Look at it honestly. Take an honest look. Then if there is something for us to discuss as business people, I promise you, we will go ahead and discuss it."

"As people doing business," I say.

"Ah, yes, caught Homer at his nodding, did you? Yes, of course—as you say, as you say—as people doing business," says the window-shade man.

"In his nodding, I would say," I say.

"In? Yes, yes—in. Or caught out at, of course," the window-shade man says.

"So I go home?" says I to the window-shade man.

"That's it," says the window-shade man. "Unless it is your wish," says the window-shade man, "for us to linger over any of these imponderables of ours."

"Perhaps upon the occasion of my return," says I.

Says the window-shade man, "Should you choose for there to be one, that is. For there is the shop up or down the block," says the window-shade man.

Says I, "But it goes with me or stays here?"

Says the window-shade man, "You mean this window shade here. You mean while you go elsewhere, do you leave this window shade here."

"Home," says I. "Home only," says I. "Not elsewhere at all," says I.

"I don't know," says the window-shade man. "It is for you as a person of reflection to resolve," says the window-shade man. "There are difficulties I cannot resolve for you," says the window-shade man.

So I says to him, "But it's decidable, you think."

The window-shade man says to me, "I think—yes, I think. But now I think no—from your point of view, it's maybe too apophantic for you."

So I says to him, "Yet mustn't something be done one way or the other?"

"You're saying this to me as conjecture?" he says.

"Am I conjecturing?" I say.

"You want to determine if you are actually, in saying what you said, formulating a conjecture," he says.

"Absolutely," says I. "But at another level, you could lock the door."

"I could come to believe business hours had come to their end," says the window-shade man.

"Where's the law?" says I.

Says he, "Belief and the law, you're saying to me belief and the law, they cannot be tessellated?"

"Friendly relations, it makes for friends?" says I.

"Well," says the window-shade man, "extensity and intensity, there's always all that, isn't there?"

"Scum-sucking swine," says I. "Grommetless dog."

"Not grommetless, sir!" asserts the window-shade man. "Never been proved grommetless!" asserts the window-shade man.

"Point," says I. "Therefore," says I, "speak not to me of gussets," says I.

"But see you, don't you see you," says the window-shade man, calmer not by half but by much, "that are we not, in this matter, made claimants, then, the pair of us, on common but nonrelational ground?"

"Good," says I to the window-shade man.

"Which makes this mine," says I to the window-shade man, leaving the window shade to keep to its place in the hands of the window-shade man and plucking the fascia from the face of the window-shade man, no more himself a window-shade man than I a shopper in want of even infrequent dark.

EXCELSIOR

Granted, he went down to a tumor in the bowel. Also granted, chances are he wouldn't have gotten that cancer down there if he had not always had a bottle of J.T.S. Brown in his big hand whenever we went grousing around for those little like newborn flounder and fluke in the local waters where the undergrowth was bound to foul whichever growth of engine you had, which in Uncle Charlie's case was not a Johnson or an Evinrude and which always got the fellas working the counter at Henning's more or less sneering at him, behind his back, of course, which I can tell you is how you would have to be positioned if you had it in your head to scoff at Uncle Charlie, plus granted, he probably didn't know a lot about fishing and only had a rebuilt Mercury as the outboard he would haul to Henning's out back in the Plymouth pickup with mainly me and always Jackson and Mickey jammed up front in the cab of it with him, those vicious sonofabitching mutts already chewing at my short-pantsed knees the minute I got up there and got in there with them, filthy fat slobbering curs, they were, one a Dalmatian and the other I'm guessing a French bulldog, more defeated by obesity than what they were by age, Jackson all berserk spots and waddly belly, Mickey just thick and overgrown and mean as a snake, the pair of them shiftless as anyone ever saw a canine get, long swinging strings of rubbery drool hanging off of them like they were a breed from hell, but they could get lively enough, couldn't they, when there was me to menace and when the catch started turning up in the bucket and pails and winging out of it onto the deck. Well, they were just your regular angling buddies, Mickey and Jackson were, and you never didn't see them come along with you up in the cab of the beat-to-shit Plymouth without Uncle Charlie appearing to be in some strangely unconvincing but ruthlessly nonchalant charge of them. Goddamn, you were dumb if you couldn't right off see Uncle Charlie was nothing if not a brokenhearted man and that it was his dogs which knew it first and knew it best, yet his angry gruff presence never, to my mind, did enough to modify the raging bearing of those filthy stinking brutes of his. How Aunt Dora put up with Jackson and Mickey getting anywhere near her kitchen was a wonder and a half. Even when they were going after the bag of sandwiches the woman would have squared away for us, even before we got to Henning's, got bait, got the pails, got the bucket, got loose the rowboat Uncle Charlie had nodded at to give the boatboy to know that it was that particular rowboat that was the rowboat Uncle Charlie had come to decide in his genius was hot damn the luckiest of the tethered vessels yet to be leased of a morning, even before any of that, like getting the Mercury screwed onto the stern, getting the rods and reels and all the rest of the hodgepodgy gear in our craft, and not any of that all that thoughtfully stowed, Jackson and Mickey had stepped all over whatever remained of what they hadn't already swallowed of Aunt Dora's surplusage against the dreaded promiscuity of the bountiful sea.

Fucking animals.

You never saw anything like it, the zeal of those lumbering beasts when the edible was in view, not that I ever caught either of them nosing around the Chinese takeout cartons Henning's handed over your bait to you in. No sir, neither Jackson nor Mickey, that I ever saw, ever even so much as showed a hideous tongue to lick in curiosity the white cardboard and dare trouble the more serious species within.

Which, yes, was worms.

But bloodworms.

God yes!

In their distinctive havens with some leafy business of some arcane provenance in there with them, the vegetation, I supposed, there in reach of them for the bloodworms to be kept happy and bouncy for the uncongenial bath to come.

Let's see, what else got itself loaded into the rowboat before we used a mossy oar to pole away from the mossy dock to open water? There'd be the tackle box, skimpily furnished. The big portable radio with the big bent aerial and H. V. Kaltenborn on it or about to be on it, the war being the news of the day as of any day and H. V. Kaltenborn trusted to give it to you without unseemly mannerisms. A sweater for each of us. A first aid kit, loose aspirin, an eighth of a bottle of iodine, one standard-sized Band-Aid, the wrapper pre-torn in preparation for further, not impossibly hurried, tearing. Anything else? Weren't there always two yellow oilskins? Hang on. I'm thinking, I'm thinking—well, the dogs, of course, and Uncle Charlie himself mainly amidships except in the stern to govern the Mercury when needed, the man unwaveringly on his feet, the man already grumbling about his lumbago and what in the world was he doing offering comfort and adventure to his younger brother's goddamn rotten good-for-nothing truant of a kid who ought to have taken himself to school where he could best lend his brain and back to the general conflict. That's Uncle Charlie standing wide in the middle of the rowboat, booted feet shoved gunnel to gunnel, a whole tenth of J.T.S. Brown already sucked down and a backup tenth slipped from one of his back pockets in his hand ready for action, Aunt Dora, no fool on a Wednesday, she having had the foresight and the rachmones to lay out four tenths for the man on the kitchen counter before sunup.

Well, Uncle Charlie had all three sons in the war, didn't he?

For that matter, so did Aunt Dora, too.

But, goddamn it, his boys weren't where he wanted them to be for them to fish with him, were they?

Shit.

Off in France at some Bulge thing, to hear H. V. Kaltenborn render the idea of overseas real, all three of those boys, Big Eugene, Kenny, Abby.

You know what just this instant occurred to me? Damn it, bet you Uncle Charlie never even knew my name—except perhaps to say, if pressed, my brother Phillie's kid.

Abby he called Flubber.

I was jealous of that.

Don't worry, they all three of them got back all right, though maybe not, after that, so right after all.

The war, to my mind, was fabulous excitement.

I collected newspaper and cooking grease and longed for the restoration of Fleer's Dubble Bubble Gum, initial caps, damn it, yes!

Uncle Charlie, however, and Aunt Dora, they must have both of them known what war was. Me too, am I right? It was fun. War was fun.

At the moment, we piddled along to our spot, the renovated Mercury pushing us ever so timidly into the patch of water, call it, we called it "the channel," where the hunting was always hot, Uncle Charlie fairly plastered by now as he justly intended, his stance still steady enough, the father of sons standing wide in America, boots arranged athwart and so on, if any of these words can be felt to actually apply to this nautical remembrance, mishap, shambling distraction from everything H. V. Kaltenborn was worrying all about in our behalf.

We'd get to the shade of the bridge, taking meticulous care not to drift out from under it off to the other side, where the true sea was, and danger—weather and tumult and God knew what, certainly the terrible deep. Uncle Charlie would let the puny anchor down, test the rope, make certain we were secure, safe from unspeakable forces—German agents floating all about asquat in balloon tubes, German U-boats poking around for uncles and nephews as hostages ripe for the snatching.

We were canny, prudent, unimpeachably cautious.

I was afraid.

I also always sensed I was only instants from my having to yield to the command of number two. I held myself rigid with expectation, at any second I was going to be unable but to surrender to the anguish surmounting all other imperatives. Not for a minute did I succeed in concentrating on the assault at hand. It wasn't really wanted yet. I mean, Uncle Charlie handled the hunt. I fitted myself into the cubby of the prow, probably shivering from fear, the crotch of the short pants crowding my miserable putz, the vermin with tails and four feet to the good glaring at me and my tenderness out of their satanic vile eyes.

My friend, we were jiggling in the murk of "the channel."

Wasn't it time for us to try our luck? Yes, Uncle Charlie was smashed, pixilated, gone—had already released two empties into the easeless sea—but the man never flinched. He baited me up, stuck a finger into one of the cartons, withdrew from it an extraordinarily lengthsome and chubby bloodworm, flicked some green crap off it into Jackson's face, and there we were, lines bobbing in the oily water, a third tenth in Uncle Charlie's free hand, his other hand, knife gripped oddly, a sort of sidesaddle style, slicing sections of bloodworm for us in vast anticipation of spreading the wealth, the cutting board—honest, no shit—the meaty thigh of his coverall, or is it plural?

Man oh man, my uncle was drunk and we were, albeit not at sea actually but, yes, yes, in water depthsome enough for us to ply the mysterious fecundity of the channel, and were doing it, two Lish men and their faithful companions, standing wide as best we could, the baby fluke and the baby flounder flying into our hands as if by deviltry. And so it was, and then it was, that I think I might have heard the father of those sons importuning the heavens for Flubber and his brothers to come right straight home, whatever difficulties H. V. Kaltenborn was on the airwaves warning of.

"Bull-floppy!" I believe I heard my uncle shout. "Battle of the Bulge, fucking froggie bull-floppy!" The man observing the courtesy of turning his voice away from me as he stood wide-stanced in the middle of the rowboat, saluting the other boats with his third tenth held high, then bending himself down double to me for him to thread anew a fresh slab of bloodworm on my hook, the gruesome things bunching up in clots and gouts of innards, recoiling from the point of the hook, then relaxing into a narrowed bleached desuetude as some tranche of themselves was skidded up the steel and around the curve, or curl, into place.

You know the word aduncous?

Didn't I once see that in a dictionary?

Aduncous?

Listen, I understood my cousins were not where they wanted to be, nor where their father would have them be if he were the ruler of all. Uncle Charlie wanted Big Eugene and Kenny and

Abby in the boat with him, although I can't imagine more than one of the boys and his father would fit in it any of them both at once. As for me, there was no joy in all this. I was glad to escape school, but afraid of everything else—the worms, the dogs, the fish, the water, the countermen at Henning's, and especially Uncle Charlie. But, truth, I wanted to grow up to be exactly like the man and parade around town with fierce dogs at my side like that, drink till skunked, operate a Mercury rebuilt, handle a knife, handle bait, be a father, handle a heart breaking for want of sons.

I suppose you could say they were where the spooky ocean was, whereas we would never venture anywhere close to it. No reason to. What we were hunting, as fishermen hunt, was the illegal stuff, the baby flounder and the baby fluke, which you could pluck up out of the unpleasant moil three at a time on a single hook. Just drop your rig in until you felt the sinker tap the bottom, take up the line half a turn, then wait for the payoff—which you would have evidence of in two shakes, tiny newborn fish coming hard and fast, so long as you didn't forget to keep wiggling and bobbing your line a little and not doze off.

This was the seaman's godawful struggle as far as I could see from our point of view.

It was murder.

Which even in those crummy waters was felonious and shameful and wonderfully, wonderfully fulfilling.

But no sweat.

Never saw fish and game wardens on duty. Probably were off in the service themselves.

To me, the measly fish were lousy Germans, and their captor and his mate were getting even for Uncle Charlie's Big Eugene and Kenny and Abby and the whole United States. But there were some bad aspects to it too. Okay, I'll lay them out for you. One, there was how to take a leak when at sea. Two, there was hoping you didn't have to, as I think I may have mentioned, do number two. Which would have to be in the bucket if you did have to do it, or in one of the pails, I always supposed, a prospect impossible for me to realize, however conceived, given my dainty nature. Besides, the bucket filled up in no time at all, as did the pails, used as they all of them were to hold the catch as we caught it, until there was nowhere for the perishing infants to be slid into anymore and, good Christ, look out, they'd start flipping themselves out of their on-board habitats and flood, if that's the word, the deck, if that's one also, and the bottom of the boat would be all aclutter with madly breathing things, all frantic gills, like gasping, let's say, but definitely dying anyway, dying, dying, all of it going on everywhere all around you—death plus the fucking rumpus death made, which was where I would come in, getting off my backside in the prow, getting myself squatted on my haunches, and, taking up the—no, wait.

Haven't set the stage for it yet, have I?

First of all, I'm crouched as far from Jackson and Mickey as I can manage myself to get. Second, I have my orders from the commodore, the commander, the captain, him.

What?

You know what!

Quiet the catch!

Or words to that effect, for which task Henning's supplied a variety of tools.

Truncheon.

Nightstick.

Blackjack.

Pry bar.

Junior-sized baseball bat.

Iron elbow.

Wrench.

Hammer handle.

Ax handle.

Hammer.

Ax.

Just remembered where Uncle Charlie finagled the imperative from.

Stand wide!

It was how Flubber signed off his V-mails from the Front.

I mean it when I say the Front, okay?

You get it when I say the Front?

To Aunt Dora too, of course—but I never was present when Aunt Dora had to steady herself, sturdy herself, to face the unfaceable day. Not that I didn't, however, see the woman after Sunday meals at Uncle Charlie's and Aunt Dora's, while the pair of briskets lay ravaged on the table and it was only the littlest cousins who had hung back to pick at the meat. Oh, sure, there was rationing and all that, but this was Uncle Charlie we're talking about and didn't he have gasoline for the Mercury and lots more of it for the Plymouth? Meat on the table was a godsend, wasn't it, even if God hadn't thought to send it.

Man oh man, I'm eighty-six now and I'm still willing to claim no meat was ever in all my life so tasty.

Stand wide! Your loving son, Flubber.

Big Eugene married Edna, the girl next door. It was annulled a month later. Then Big Eugene married Norma, the first Gentile to show up in the family accords, and a divorced person too, fancy that. Kenny also married a woman named Norma, from Brooklyn, but somehow, nevertheless, in unforgettable possession of an English accent blended, no, not blended but heathered, with the

Brooklyn one. Then there was Abby, the youngest and the prize, who goes to West Point after France, then takes as wife the daughter of a big-time lumber guy, rich, rich, you never heard the end of it, so rich. Ugly too. Leila, or anyhow Lila—I don't know the spelling but that was the essence of the name. It wrecked his life, I believe we may safely say, and then Flubber goes ahead and wrecks it worse—with a second wife whom Abby's three sons, they right away commence to refer to as Shloink, the Shloink—a true horror, which I hear all about from Abby's youngest son, Peter, and Peter's Gentile wife, whose name a moment ago I just forgot. It was set, the nuptials were, in the House of the Redeemer, in the block back behind the one where I live, Peter and Jim and Andy, sons, sons all wearing top hats and so on and so forth.

A touch of the Jewish thing.

Hats like that.

Of course in years hence I hear all about how the guy of greatest promise—Flubber, that is—would pound these three boys of his with his fists, if you can believe it.

No shit.

My friend, I saw those fists, or anyhow Abby's wrists.

Never saw a man with thicker wrists, did I?

Or worse rages—unless they were Uncle Charlie's.

But all that stuff, that all belongs to an entirely different setup. Just mentioned it here to keep you from thinking the worst came about overseas. But I suppose you can say that it might have, yet never did I hear a single murmur of Big Eugene or Kenny going wacko. Big Eugene, he went South and got himself into the sock business. Kenny worked on oil in Venezuela until they kicked him out and then the H-bomb. Abby, the man was later on as happy as a clam in high water with his Shloink and all that.

Life in the long lens, or is it through it?

You know.

Listen—don't look.

Strange. Who knows? Such a good guy—until he wasn't.

Those wrists, I'll tell you this—they were Uncle Charlie's, big, scary, hairy hands. Oh boy. No counterman at Henning's, though it cannot be but that they thought it, came anywhere near to letting you hear kike said when the little posse of us came in the door. Pie-eyed as the man mostly was, you wouldn't hope to trifle with him over pettinesses like who's a Yid and who's not, especially when the cancer started really hunkering down and eating him in big bites. In the rowboat rented and poled out from the dock at Henning's, the man would just keep standing the whole time going out, and once out there, in the channel, say, he never got off his feet. I saw Uncle Charlie die like that, an inflatable tube under his tuchus to deliver the impression balm was at hand.

But it wasn't.

He stood wide, all right, just as I did when, thoroughly pissed, Uncle Charlie would issue me my orders.

What were they?

I already told you!

Quiet the catch?

Subdue the catch?

Something faintly humorous, no?

And I'd come all of the way out of my cranny (hey, let's call it foxhole) and take the lethal utensil he passed to me and, scruffing around crab-like, I'd patrol the deck for gills ever so slightly atremble and bash the fuckers dead—much as I had no stomach for it and would swear to the fact in my nightly prayers before I even had said God bless Mother and God bless Daddy and so on and so forth, imploring the Lord for forgiveness for my killing things.

I was no killer, and am still not. So far, anyway.

Yet, man alive, how I'd go for the eats at breakfast the next morning!

Friend, pay attention, it was my job.

On board.

The big-looking man at the helm had, in a manner of speaking, spoken.

Silence, for pity's sake, for my head is splitting here!

It's true.

Well, be quiet!

It's you who's in the catch now, no?

I beat the life out of those newborns brought up shrieking from the shallow depths, rooching myself along the bottom of the rowboat in the blood and the muck and the slobber and the gunk the doomed fish produced with big assists from Mickey and Jackson, the bastards knocking each other aside for them to squeeze their massive guts past one another and get at the food.

It was awful.

But I'd be leaving out the best part if I didn't tell you they made for the best eating ever, those little itsy-bitsy stolen baby fish, abducted, carried off, kidnapped.

The best.

Tops.

Get them home. Distribute shares to the neighbors. Leave the skin on, leave the bones in, fiddle the ick out—hack the heads off, get them fishkelehs in grease in the fry pan, man oh man, that was eating, fressing, not Dora's brisket but, anyway, real food.

Heavenly.

That's the word.

Got to admit it, easily the treat of my childhood and, now at eighty-six, I yearn for the return if only of the memory and the figment of happiness that comes with it.

I mean of tasting something.

Anything.

A fish fry to stir your fondest remembrances of all your nights and days.

And no school.

I'm not shitting you.

That was good living, wartime, with Uncle Charlie missing his boys and training me to try standing as wide as Flubber said he was.

Plus could.

That's the whole story right there—except to say on Sundays many's the time I would go over to Uncle Charlie's house on Kerrytown Road and sit in the kitchen and watch Aunt Dora working the briskets and the rest, the potatoes, spuds, gravy, all that, and seeing her, after the family hurly-burly, taking up her place at a window in the living room and gazing out at the yard in front or at whatever it was that always held her interest fastened there on one spot like that—until you'd quit looking and go back to the table and pick at more brisket some more and maybe start a fight with any cousin littler than you.

Twice, however, I heard.

Like a sigh, I'd say it was.

The woman wiping her hands on her apron even though her hands always looked dry and clean, Aunt Dora just taking her time to keep looking out at the world like that, just an ordinary yard, the woman not otherwise moving or doing anything, until she'd sigh this inimitable kind of Jewish sigh of hers that she had, starting up high and coming down the scale in spurts like, you might say, like just this absolute exhalation thing, letting it all out, in rhythm, don't you know it!—all the air in the heart of her, and voicing some of it as it went, with maybe a little snuffle in it, yeah, definitely, sure—like unh unh unh.

I loved it.

I tell you, I fucking loved it, that sigh of Aunt Dora's.

Mind you, I wouldn't say it was Aunt Dora getting rid of anything but maybe of her exercising her soul on account of its having some colossal unutterable knowledge in it in there.

Like this.

No, I'd never get it right.

But you really, I think, you might want to try it yourself sometime.

It's funny and sad—as the poet is forever noting, both styles at once.

It's a very Jewish thing, I'd insist—at least to my ear, it is.

Pealing down from up on high—soft, not loud, very gentle, gently, thoroughly complicit, a speechless recognition of what it's all about—all her life kept to herself all in secret.

Wish like the dickens I could get it in print for us.

But I hear it the clearest of anything, is all.

Goddamn you people, can't you ever really listen for once!

A shuddering, a decrescendo, call it, a kind of unswallowable afflatus, or is it deflatus, concessive but somehow triumphant.

Vey ist mir.

Well, hell, they're all of them long dead now, the lot of those old-time Lishes I've mentioned, not to also mention plenty of their kids gone everywhere too. But Aunt Dora's peculiar sigh or song or sign of unappeased unexcelled exhaustion, seasoned with confidential smarts plus cunning irresistance, believe me, I've got it to this day down cold down inside of me, I swear, unless it is truer to say down in me down cold.

INTO THE BARGAIN

Here's a bit for you. It's an impressive one too. My bet is you are going to be really refreshingly impressed with it, or by it, which I have to tell you is what I myself was when the woman involved in the event disclosed her heart to me. First, as to setting—temporal, spatial, all that. So, fine, so the thing starts maybe all of an hour ago just a block from where I am sitting right this minute typing this up for you to read it and get out of it the same kick I did. She types too—the woman. She is always typing, is my understanding—or was, back when I used to see her somewhat, let us just fancy, social-wise. As a matter of fact, when I said to her, "What's up? I mean what are you doing here in this neighborhood? Do you have a pass, were you issued a pass, a license maybe, any style of a permit you can show me authorizing you to come up here into this restricted district of mine?" she laughed. I think she thought I was trying to be funny. Let me tell you something—that's the one thing I never try to be—namely, funny. No, no, I was just doing what I could to maybe get away with having to snoggle for the usual sort of talk, lay on her a smart-aleck greeting of a sort, which apposition I only went to the bother of just now constructing so I could say sort and sorts, repeating and repeating stuff to stuff the insidious silence with insidious sound, however otiose or bootless or inutile dexterity appears (to be?) *on the surface.* You get what I'm getting at?—the stressing of the effect of there being something sly down beneath down under things as regards below the surface, see? But which surface, eh wot? Or, anyway, surface of exactly what, eh wot? (You see? Can't help myself. It's like this thing I've got which is like an irresistibly compulsive thing.) Oh, boy, I am all of a sudden so tired. I, Gordon, son of Reggie, am all of a sudden so suddenly utterly all in, just fucking pooped. Like, you know, like weary, wearied, *ausgespielt* if you're German, right? Nap. But, hey, before I fall and hit my head, I'm just going to go ahead and take myself a little teensy tiny nap, fair enough? Be back in a shake, I promise.

Mmm, nice. Told you I'd be right back. So there. Good as my word. Plus, feeling ten thousand percent. Nothing like sleep, let me tell you. Anyway, as I was going to say to you, small talk, the ceremonial, it gets me jumpy and tongue-tied, see?—especially when there's the blam of a city smashing the nuclei of your cochlea from all four sides of your brain. Or, okay, six. I mean, the street. Knocking yourself out to make a show of confecting coherent conversation on the street, okay? This was the street. Or, fine, on the street. Or *in* it—since as for *on*, we were, the scene was taking place, the one consisting in this woman and I, *on* the sidewalk. But I may have already said so, mayn't I have? Anyway, I was aiming for home from marketing and here she was, the woman I am telling you about, making her way along the sidewalk, coming right dead-on at me, a woman I, Gordon, had not, I swear to you, laid eyes on in a shockingly long time. Some beauty too. A real knockout. But in her years, of course, not in the slightest other than I. That's right—we're old. Okay, so this woman laughs a little and she says to me, "I was at the school—went by for a used-book sale at the school."

"Really?" I say. "At the school, you say? Buy anything?" I say. "Oh, just these," she says, spreading open the dainty shopping bag she's hauling with her and giving me a peek inside. There's two books in there. I finger them around, trying to get it to look as if I'm earnestly interested in getting a look, and see, yeah, yeah, just crap, more crap, writing, writing, etc. and so on. "Sophie, this is crap," I says to her, and she says, abashed is the word, or embarrassed, "I know, I know." So I says to her, "Sophie, will you please explain yourself? I am waiting to hear you make a forceful enough attempt to explain yourself," which, you know, gets another laugh out of her, but she touches my arm, the way you do, and I do ditto to hers, and this part of it is really honestly terrific for me because, don't make me have to say it to you again, this person is, old as she is, a really terrifically classy type of a looker. "And you?" she says. "Because I never see you on the street anymore—oh, but probably it's me—always hatching up dreams at home by reason of beating my keyboard to death."

"Um, not me," I say. "Quit it all just after the wife died. It's not for me anymore, all of that maddening shit, verbs and nouns and worse. What I do," I says to her, "is I keep myself frantically busy fussing with the place."

"Is that so?" the woman, tired and tiresomely, says.

"Seems to be," I say, and can see this powwow half a lick from a ghastly stall, and, thus, high time for everybody's sake to make all speed for a semi-graceful goodbye and let us please get going on our separate ways.

I touch her arm.

It's nice. Like sleep.

"Got to giddyap," I say. "Projects."

"Oh?" she says. "Like what?" she says.

Well, you can see how it is—one, I don't want to be outdone, take off with the question, with *her* question, still in charge of the verbal situation which had been developing on the street just more or less just moments ago, which would be, if I did it, did yield, did give way, did fail to return reply, it would be like my giving this person the, you know, the victory, you might not inappropriately say, yes—and, two—two, I all of a sudden figure there's maybe more to be said for touching hastening on the way in the offing for me here, so sexily, you might say, I says to the woman, "Ah, you know, just puttering around with my place, keeping things up to grade—or is it code?—doing what I can so the wife does not have to rest in everlasting shame."

"Barbara?" the woman says.

"That's right," I say. "Good of you to remember the name. And Howard?" hoping and praying it's me who's this time remembering right (unless it's aright), that it's not John or something, Alphonse or Gray. "Pretty tough still, is it, or are you actually getting yourself settled in with all of the adjustments and all?"

"Yes, Howard," she says, and looks off up into the wild blue yonder and, still gazing away, says to me, "Projects you said? Such as what?" she says to me, saying to me, after her saying just that little bit to me, not one other word, not nought, by Christ—until I, Gordon, am standing there with her on the sidewalk with her all talked out, not having shown this person up, I should certainly say, not having exhibited to this person just what fucking grief is all about, which is when the woman gives me a look and says to me, touching my arm again *into the bargain*, "Oh, Gordon, you are such a tease," and keeps touching my arm, keeps her hand in noticeably secure touch with my arm, in the manner of somebody determined to hold a person stationed right there where the two of them, persons the pair of them, are—as in don't leave, don't leave, and, sighing, saying to me, she says to me, "I know, I know—it's exactly the same with me." And here it happens, I can tell it, I can tell it, this woman is going to come at me with a comeback, goddamn it—I took too stuporously long trying to think up some sort of a reportable project—the mattress, the bed skirt, the phone in the kitchen sticky with its locale in the vicinity of lots of lonely frying.

But it's crazy how I remember it.

His pipe. The man's pipe. Her husband's pipe, which I, Gordon, first apprehends as a pipe, as just a fucking pipe, as just the prop for a man named Howard, isn't it, type of chap for him to sport a pipe, hah!

"Oh," she murmurs to me, getting herself right in close to my face, "but isn't one forever thinking of it—Howard's favorite pipe?"

Me, I told her about some stuff I couldn't seem to shut up about—the mattress, the bed skirt, the kitchen telephone. "Oh," she says, "isn't it what always so heartbreakingly happens when you don't buy bedding at a department store where if you don't, then you don't have any, not the least, latitude as to any recourse of return, or last resort to it, or for credit? Gordon," the woman says to me, admonishing me, and not at all soothingly, "don't tell me Barbara never advised you to keep yourself well out of the reach of the specialty shops!"

I think I said, "Latitude?"

I think I may have said, "Latitude?"

You can lose the thread, you know.

You can lose it even if it's your own textile you're weaving.

Jesus, I am so goddamn tired again. Oh, man, am I . . . beat! Do you ever get to feel like this? You know what I mean? But maybe you don't. Maybe you're different from me. But maybe you're not like her, either. I mean, I'm thinking a pipe pipe—like a briar pipe, right? But you know what in just mere minutes from then I'm willing to grant? And, hey, listen, I'm prepared to insist it's a sign of growth in me, isn't it?—this recent willingness I just mentioned to you where I'm willing to grant somebody a little something by way of exoneration—as in maybe a little benefit of the doubt.

"Sophie," I says to her, tap-tapping the handier of her elbows with my two happy fingers working in synchrony. Still, doing this pretty consolingly, you do, I trust, understand—tap, tap, tap, gently, gently. I says to her, "Sophie, do you actually mean for me to interpret your meaning as meaning like a pipe in the basement or something—not something like a Meerschaum, right? But, you know, instead—instead an overhead pipe, industrial and all that?"

"Well," she says (Sophie says to me, Gordon, you do continue to see), "dear Howard, dearest Howard, he had, I have to tell you, the man had picked out a big green heating pipe he felt very protective about."

Or of, I, for the record, corrected—but, uncharacteristically, keeping my annoyance to myself.

Fuck it. You probably know how it goes from here—her getting me, with a touch and a half, to go with her over to her place to see it down there in her building's basement—some superintendent's gardener's glossy high-class green. Then I, of course, got her to come hurry right over with me to my place and, you guessed it, showed her, I showed her, absolutely—well, yes—every dazzling detail.

Which is to say the sole project left to me.

Oh hell, the one, to be fair, left to the legion of both of us, I suppose it's, inescapably, only virtuous for me to allow.

GRACE

I am writing this the night of 30 January 1994.

Barbara is in the next room.

She is being fed by two nurses. One spoons the soupy food onto Barbara's tongue, the other promptly pushes between Barbara's teeth the canula that carries what Barbara cannot swallow down into the canister where what is suctioned out of Barbara's mouth is stored until someone must come dump the contents into the bedroom toilet so that the procedure might be continued without spillover or mechanical breakdown.

Barbara will be fed, in this manner, all night, which means, as a rule—all night, that is—until about four in the morning, at which time Barbara will be prepared for bed, and then finally laid down onto it at about six thirty. She will be gotten up from bed and positioned back into her chair, this in the care of three shifts of a pair of nurses who come to us as Mercy Persons, until about four in the morning of 31 January—if, in fact, there is going to be a 31 January this year.

I don't know.

I turn sixty in February.

I mention these matters not to press you with the force of conditions now in sway in Barbara's life but instead to create the context for the one literary memoir—if this is what it might be claimed this recollection of mine is—I am ever likely to impart to print.

It concerns the critic Frank Lentricchia and the novelist Cynthia Ozick.

It concerns eating.

It concerns an item that belonged to Barbara but which I took from Barbara—actually, from the chifforobe in the room Barbara now sits in now being fed in as I now sit writing in this one—the evening last July when Ozick and Lentricchia asked me to come out to dinner with them.

It was, the item, vintage spectacles that pinch the nose to keep themselves stationed at their post and that have a ribbon that, looped through an eyelet formed from the frame, goes over the head and takes purchase around the neck and hangs down.

Pince-nez, yes?

Barbara never wore them.

The glass in them was plain glass.

I had picked up this novelty for Barbara from some sort of fashion emporium back when we were first setting up housekeeping together.

The pince-nez were like so many of the things I was then snatching from everywhere for Barbara—notions I had, frenzied notions, of ornamenting her, of delineating her, in her beauty.

Barbara was a very beautiful woman.

Barbara is still, inexpressibly, incredibly—reduced to a depletion more severe than anything I would have imagined possible without death present in complete dominion—a very beautiful woman. You can see this, Barbara's authority in this category, registering in the styles of approach made to her by the women who come to nurse Barbara—a sort of recognition, I think it is, a sort of satisfied acknowledgement of the insult nature reserves—just-ly!—for the very beautiful.

Barbara is regnant in there in our bedroom with two such nurses right now. They feed her, or struggle to feed her, as Barbara, for her part, struggles to swallow little sips of what was yesterday cooked and pureed for her, everybody in there, none more blindingly beautiful than Barbara herself, getting a good look at what most of us never see: the work that can be done to the body by amyotrophic lateral sclerosis.

Lou Gehrig's disease.

But what I want to tell you about is about another experience in eating and about other persons—and about, please remember, the pince-nez.

Which last I had taken from the top drawer of Barbara's chifforobe in order that I might feel I was in prospect of holding my own—as a full-fledged participant—in the company of Lentricchia and Ozick the night of the dinner I am remarking.

I took them with me, the pince-nez, for just that reason—or for no reason that I can honorably say.

I don't know.

Say that I had been in all day, been in for days, had not been out of the house—not at night, anyway—for weeks and weeks—and had certainly not been out for anything social in months, months, months.

Lentricchia and Ozick, Ozick and Lentricchia.

They—one or the other of them—phoned, said come out to dinner with us, said come meet us in an hour at the Grand Ticino, said come look for it just north of Bleecker on Thompson.

I said yes, yes, oh yes, hung up the phone, went with tears in my eyes—it's crazy—to the bedroom, to the chifforobe, took out the pince-nez, got my shoe trapped under one of the canulas or catheters or electric cords everywhere underfoot, got the shoe loose, went to the bookshelves, took down Ozick's *Bloodshed*, took down Lentricchia's *Ariel and the Police*, went to the kitchen, made out a note for the nurses then on duty and for those to come on at ten, said I'd be back no later than eleven, added the telephone number where I could be reached, and went, left, fled, took myself out into the street in the temper of one released.

Now to the little joke in this.

What I know I called a memoir but can now see will never accumulate itself into anything so grand, and God knows into nothing anywhere on speaking terms with something traveling under papers as a literary one.

It's just a bit.

I can tell it to you, the whole bit, in no time flat.

They were late.

I sat there being exasperated with them.

Why were they late?

Wasn't I on time? What right did they have to be late when there I was—right when they said I should be—right on fucking time? And what right did they have to make it up between them that we, that the three of us, would come eat at the Grand Ticino when—fuck, fuck!—doors away, also just north on Thompson off Bleecker, was Porto Bello—where with Bloom, with Donoghue, where with Ozick and Lentricchia—where all the years with Barbara, goddamn it!—I had had such good times, such happinesses—releases to, not releases from.

I tried thinking of topics.

Then I was glad of it, glad for it—glad the dirty fucking rats, the bums, were late.

Because I did not have anything to talk with them about—no topics, not a topic—did not have anything to say for myself, did not feel anything in me sufficient in worth to swap for the gift of anyone's time with me—except to hand these people my tears again in thanks again for their thinking again to ask me to come out with them for eats again.

I had one topic.

Barbara.

Barbara dying.

So I sat there being exasperated a little bit, and weeping a little bit, and being pleased with myself for the pince-nez hanging zanily from my neck and for the copy of *Bloodshed* and for the copy of *Ariel and the Police* I had thought to pack along with me for no motive I could state to you with any more good sense backing it up than I could summon in defense of myself for my getting myself primped up with the pince-nez.

I thought: Tell them I'd just made up my mind my favorite sentence is Edward Loomis's "Mary Rollins was born in a high white frame house shaded by elms."

I thought: Tell them I am getting ready to make my second-favorite sentence "The icepack has melted, and the American River is running fast."

I thought: Do I tell them it's mine, this sentence—ah, shit, compound sentence!—or tell them instead that all I really did was steal it from where it was scribbled up on some wall somewhere?

I thought: Tell them I've got money in my pocket and I'm going to get bad drunk and then get on a bus, get on any bus, so long as it's going away.

I thought: Tell them I'm pretty damn burnt up they didn't deal me in when they didn't settle on good old Porto Bello.

I thought: Tell them they're my first- and my second-best friends?

I sat there thinking.

I sat there thinking, sat there waiting, sat there making believe I was actually reading the books I had laid out in my lap when I had pushed back my chair back away from the table when the waiter had come and had put a cup of espresso in front of me and had filled the bread basket with some great-looking bread in it for me and had poured out for me a little dish of olive oil for me, and had, in every ordinary thing the fellow had done for me, in every conventional ministration the waiter had enacted for me, that the man had—the strictness, the covenant with protocol—got the tears to come from me again, carried me into a sort of small weeping again—so that, sure, sure, I guess I could not actually have sat there reading anything even if I had actually been trying to.

I sat there thinking: Hey, what do they make of me, the other people back behind me in this place, me, this pose-taker I am, this show-person sitting here, the ridiculous specs stuck to the nose, the broad black grosgrain ribbon swagged martially across the chest, the legs arranged at an important three-quarter torque, the auspicious-looking books laid out in the lap, the chair shoved back away from the table in an exhibition of a sort of magisterial, expansive remove?

I sat there thinking: Where the piss are they, the dirty stinking rats, not to be here now, not for them to see me looking like this now, not for them to be right this instant coming up on me from the back of me seeing me looking like this now?

I'm ready! Please see me now—I'm ready!

But are the bastardos here and ready for them to do the fucking viewing?

I sat thinking: Tell them about how on my way downtown I spotted on Broadway between Twenty-Second and Twenty-First a store called G O R D O N with a sign saying something like, wasn't it, *Sells Tricks, Sells Novelties, Sells Disguises*?

I thought: Tell them they are the both of them both my first-best friends as friends?

I thought: Tell them they made me cry?

I thought: Tell them everything makes me cry?

I thought: Tell them I put on a dirty movie when Barbara was sleeping or when I thought Barbara was sleeping and there was a girl in it getting it from all sides in it but who never once looked at any of the ones giving it to her in it but who instead was only always looking off somewhere away from where everything was going on in the holes in her as if—in a gaze, in a gaze!—where she looked off to was paradise?

I thought: Tell them, of the three chairs, that of the three chairs, that I, Gordon, was the first one here first but that I, Gordon, of the three chairs, that I took the one chair facing to the back, took the one chair facing to the kitchen, because what wouldn't I, Gordon, not do for my two first-best friends if not eat shit for them, if not face the kitchen doing it for them?

I thought: Tell them I took the pince-nez when Barbara wasn't looking, tell them I never told Barbara I was taking them, tell them I couldn't really read with them, tell them I wasn't really reading with them, tell them they didn't have anything but just plain glass in them, tell them I am not going to be ashamed of any of this, tell them I am not going to be ashamed of anything anywhere to do with any of this, tell them no, no, not if at least, not if I, Gordon, can at least be somewhere on time at least when I am goddamn told to be at least and they—the bastardos!—can't!

In the midst of which consideration I take up a big piece of the bread up from the bread basket and tear off a little piece of it from the big piece and put the little piece down into the little dish of olive oil and soak the little piece of bread with olive oil and then take up the salt shaker and salt the oiled bread with salt and put the little piece of salted, oiled bread into my mouth and start chewing and keep chewing and then take up the cup of espresso and take a sip from the cup of espresso and sit chewing and sit posing and sit making believe I am sitting reading but sit really actually just thinking—fuck, fuck—this fucking bread here is pretty fucking good bread here, this bread here at the Grand Ticino is pretty fucking good bread here—and just getting more bread, getting it all salted, getting it all oiled, getting more of the coffee into my mouth, getting the whole glob of it all good and chewed and soaked and mashed, thinking: Tell the bastardos what, what?

I think: Tell them there are Mercy Persons coming to us from Saint Firmus, tell them there are Mercy Persons coming to us from Saint Eustatius.

I think: Tell them there is no person merciful enough coming to anyone from anywhere.

I think: Proust! I think: That's it, Proust!

What a topic, Proust—the bum, the bum, the stinking dirty rat, forgetting the cookie, and whose damn cookie is it but the braggart's own damn cookie!

Tell them the filth can't even remember to remember his own damn cookie, can't even damn remember to remember not even three little pages hence concerning naught but remembering, can't even, goddamn it, remember it's the two of them, that it's the totality of the two of them, that it is the totalitarian unicity of the blend of the savors of the two fucking two of them that authorizes the emancipation of anything, that it's the tea *and* the cookie, that it's the tea now and now the cookie now, that it's the both of them now, this reciprocation, goddamn it!

Tell them I think.

Tell them the instant they show up that I think.

And then I think Holy God Jesus, how about asphyxiation for a topic!

Because it is all of a sudden fucking occurring to me I am fucking sitting here in fucking the Grand Ticino fucking strangling!

I mean it, I mean it!—I have gone and got a lump of oily salty coffeed-up mush that's gone and got itself caught halfway down and will not go anymore down than halfway down anymore because there is laid out beneath it this swag of big broad black grosgrain ribbon I somehow got caught in under the bread when I was sticking the fucking bread in my mouth and then got the ribbon halfway swallowed down under the bread and it's hung up on me halfway down, like this bundle of it, like this terrible bag of it, and it won't, the whole killing sack of it, it will not come back up because it has gone too far down for it to come back up and it won't go all of the way down because my neck has got it by a rope and won't let go.

And I think: Idiot, idiot, quick, quick!—act fast before you have actually suffocated yourself!—either give it a yank and rip out your teeth or see if you can swallow your head!

That's the thought I thought.

I don't know for how long.

All I know is, hey, Barbara knows.

Legs still crossed in imperious pose, books—books!—still exhibited upon my person—while death hurries to do an honest job of it from the props bullshitting has furnished.

Okay, so that's the literary part.

The memoir part is did I or didn't I sit here and not forget that it was all of them, all?

Coffee, salt, oil, ribbon, bread.

Six, actually—actually the components constituting the effect, don't they all come, all in all, to six?

The swift convergence, fluent—calamity!—everything in your gullet at once—I can count at least to six.

And what about eyelet?

And vanity?

And canula?

But it is swell by me if you and the critic and if you and the novelist want to take the list anywhere off into your first-best schemes and rhymes and figures and portents.

I mean, hey, as the fella says, *reim dich oder ich fress dich*, you got it or you got it?

Except just don't go accusing anybody of ever pulling anything too Prousty on you, deal?

I said it, my darling—didn't I?

Didn't I just—he, your husband—just say deal?

COUP DE THÉÂTRE

When I was in primary school, or is it that it was in grammar school that I was in, more exactly, more on-the-nose-ish-ly, in the eighth grade thereof, I performed the role of Rafe in the Gilbert and Sullivan operetta *H.M.S. Pinafore*.

Sylvia Wachsburger played the part of the captain's daughter and Janice Birnbaum played the part of Buttercup, and I, Gordon, took myself, not as Rafe the tar but as Gordo the star, to be beauteously maddened out of my tree for both of them, but marked, however, by such an abundance of lucklessness as to bar me forever from my ever once savoring the seasoning reaching my clichéd senses from the newly christened crotches of my co-religionists, there in the blazing ravelment of their thespian allure. Thus it was with doubled piquance that I, Gordon—Gordo!—flared my nostrils and proposed to the rabble assembled in the school's assembly hall the song of my ravishing heartbreak of stage-craftedly shocked resignation.

Farewell, my own, light of my life, farewell—for crimes unknown I go to my dungeon cell.

I sang not to Wachsburger nor to Birnbaum, but with all my deceit to naught but the parents and teachers.

Unless it was to the teachers and parents that I sang.
It was long ago.

Thus.
Oh, hark!
Oh, harken!
I ask for no more than that you please just listen.
*Farewell, my own, light of my life, farewell—for crimes unknown
I go to my dungeon cell.*

You heard every word?
Attenday every word?

Farewell, my own, light of my life, farewell—

I was what?
Was I all yet of not even a teen yet but was still, *may non*, only
all of twelve years old? Think of it!—at most not even one year
more than only twelve years old, yet already reckoning so ruefully
in the matter of life and amour.

Unless I have just spelt it wrong.
Have I just spelt everything wrong?

O Jan!
O Syl!

Yesterday the age I turned when I turned yesterday the older
age I am—oh, hear me, help me!—it was yesterday eighty-four
that I just yesterday turned!

O Burger!
O Baum!

Listen, I implore you for you to just to please for just this once this one more time to please for you to please for the mercy of God to please be so good as to maybe really this one last time please actually really and truly listen.

Farewell, my own, light of my life, farewell—for crimes unknown I go to my dungeon cell.

Unless it's he goes.
Is it he who goes?
Or went?
Unless it is he who goes is what the chorus sings.
Like, you know, litaneutically?

Anyway, that was theater for me. And music for me. And amour for me. And now I am eighty-four years old, and all there is that is left for me is me.

And Percy Bysshe Shelley.

BLOOM DIES

You know what I sometimes wonder? I sometimes wonder did Harold Bloom ever get to carry out his plan for his deathbed, well, departure, call it—call it departure or farewell or, you know, last act. Because, no shit, the man told me time and again he had a performance he'd worked out for the occasion. He said how he figured it was this—they'd all be there, whoever and so on, wife, kids, students of yore, colleagues, fans, you know—bedside in attendance, each vying for Bloom's attention, each of the attendees trying to get Bloom to see he's being looked at by whomever with love insuperable, with love supernal, with the lovingest love of all, and, what you'd expect the witnesses would expect, there'd be Bloom looking back at them looking at him—but too bad for them!

Because what Bloom always liked to say was this:

That he, the death they'd all of them come to see, that what he was going to do was look away.

And face the wall!

Let me try that again.

Say it in italics.

Face the wall!

How about caps?

FACE THE WALL!

Well, turn his face to the wall is what Bloom always told me is what, or was what, he had in mind.

So what I've been wondering ever since it was in the newspaper that Bloom died is this:

Did he do that?

Did he get to do that?

Because they don't report things like that in the newspaper, do they? Plus, I certainly can't go asking anybody I'm pretty positive was there, hey, did you see that?

Did you see Harold turn away from you and face the wall?

Good gracious, you can't go asking the pertinent parties a question like that!

Back when we were friends, pals even, the man used to say to me, okay, the world is going to be turning its back on me, the world is going to be saying to me we don't need you anymore, we don't want you around anymore, so fine, I am going to turn the tables on the world and on all the people who constitute the world and just preempt the slight, is what, just beat the world at its bullshit, turn my back on it, refuse to play, face the wall—and I remember what I, Gordon, would say when Harold would say that—I'd say well, okay, do it, do it!—and Bloom would say you bet I will!—and once even elaborated on the scheme and told me that when the time came he was going to use his miraculous memory for quotation as a means of exhibiting his contempt for it all and recite Beckett's *Malone Dies* from end to end, and I said you mean from beginning to end?—and he said fine, right you are, from beginning to end—and I said with your face to the wall?—and Harold said yes, with my face to the wall—and I said but then if you're turned with your back to the whole crowd, how is your audience going to hear you spurning them, or it, catch the drift of the spurnage and so on—and he said I, Bloomo Doomo, shall hear it!

And it is my hearing it that is what matters!

That and that alone!

And I remember my saying to Bloom but what about *Molloy*? Because haven't you always told everyone, or anyhow at least told me, that it is *Molloy* which is your favorite Beckett—*Molloy* you've always said it was—*Molloy, Molloy, Molloy*?

And Harold said all right, then, very well—*Molloy* it is, or *Molloy* it shall be, I shall give them *Molloy*!

And I said give them, give them—Harold, that itself wrecks the whole idea, give them! Even the theme of give and the theme of them, they're both at odds with the essence of your scorn—and to this Bloom said Gordito my love, how right you are, I shall emend my plan, adjust it, correct it for case, and did he, I wonder, did he, I sometimes wonder, now that the man has had his chance, how did it all work out in, as it were, or was, the end? Of course, there's no way to know.

Or, rather, there is no way to know, of course.

Could I ask?

Who to ask?

Whom?

Naturally, I am not unaware many moments had to be involved for Harold to make it from end to end.

Or, say, from end to *end*.

After all, time is involved.

That's a lot of recitation.

I recall my once recommending *Krapp's Last Tape*, and twice my suggesting *Endgame*, both pieces favorites of mine.

Proposals Bloom dismissed with dismissive gestures.

Well, the fellow's memory was phenomenal.

No text, however lengthsome and complex, would prove beyond his reach. Me, I must tell you, I have no memory at all. The
simplest bit escapes me—except for some of the time some like
it hot, some like it cold, pease porridge hot, pease porridge cold,
some like it in the pot, nine days old.

Oh, lord, I think I've screwed it up.

Anyway, no matter, the point is made.

Yet let me aver I could sit forever for any of Bloom's declama-
tions, is it? As to the accuracy of his exhibitions, I'd not be the one
to interrogate on that score, would I? But I was sold.

Utterly.

The man was an exquisite exception in every respect, or make
that the respects I felt I had a handle on, which were hardly im-
mense, of course, pease-porridge-wise.

Look, for my money, it's all show business, anyway—like the
comma I just took care to get in there after business.

Okay?

I mean, nobody gets away without showing off.

Without his or her showing off?

When it comes to the wall, fine—have it your way—turn if
you can manage it. Manage to do so, is what I'm saying. Could be
pretty tough. Who knows? In my case there won't be chitchat for
shit. But I'll probably be listening, you know?

Like "You see that?"

"Sure did."

"Sonofabitch Lish did that."

"Goddamn, I saw, I saw."

"Not a word, you notice?"

"Not even the courtesy of a look."

"Gave us all the finger, did he?"

"Always told you the kook was a nut."

"Right, there's the essence of it for you."

"What essence, who essence, where essence?"

"Precisely the point."

SPEAKAGE

I said, "What is it, die?"
She said, "Who said such a thing?"
I said, "What does it mean, somebody dies?"
She said, "Never you mind, a child!"
I said, "Is it bad? Then it's bad."
She said, "What kind of child speaks to his mother like this?"
I said, "You can tell me."
She said, "Tell you, tell you—all of a sudden such words."
I said, "Then it's bad, isn't it?"
She said, "Listen to this talk from a kidlach. Be quiet. Go to sleep."
I said, "I can't 'til you tell me."
She said, "I'm your mother and I told you."
I said, "Are you trying to scare me?" I said, "You're scaring me."
She said, "To speak like this, for shame."
I said, "Do I die?"
She said, "You want to make your mother sick?"
I said, "So you know, don't you?"
She said, "What know, where know?"
I said, "Am I going to die?"
She said, "Please, the language of it. Sleep."
I said, "Who dies?"

She said, "Maybe sometimes certain people, yes."

I said, "Not everybody?"

She said, "Who is everybody?"

I said, "You, for instance—do you die?"

"Please," she said. "Shush," she said.

"Then it's true," I said.

"Enough," she said. "Sleep," she said.

I said, "Sleep? There is no sleep," I said.

"So fine," she said, "a person dies."

I said, "People, then? All of the people?"

She said, "People, what people?—it's nothing, people."

I said, "You mean everybody really?"

"Please," my mother said. "Just sleep," my mother said.

I said, "You mean you too—that you're going to die too?"

"Who doesn't die?" my mother said. "To live is to die," my mother said.

I said, "Yes, yes," I said. I said, "That's you," I said. I said, "But what about me?"

MR. GOLDBAUM

Picture Florida.

Picture Miami Beach, Florida.

Picture a shitty little apartment in a big crappy building where my mother, who is a person who is old, is going to have to go ahead and start getting used to her not being in the company of her husband anymore, not to mention not anymore being in that of anybody else who is her own flesh and blood anymore, the instant I and my sister can devise good enough alibis for us to hurry up and get the fuck out of here and go fly back up to the lives that we have been prosecuting for ourselves up in New York, this of course being before we were obliged to drop everything and get down here yesterday in time to ride along with the old woman in the limo which had been set up for her to take her to my dad's funeral.

It took her.

It took us and her.

Meaning me and my sister with her.

Then it took us right back here to where we have been sitting ever since we came back to sit ourselves down and wait for neighbors to come call—I am checking my watch—about nine billion minutes ago.

Picture nine minutes in this room.

Or just smell it, smell the room.

Picture the smell of where they lived when it was the both of them who lived, and then go ahead and picture her smelling to see if she can still smell him in it anymore.

I am going to give you the picture of how they walked—always together, never one without the other, her always the one in front, him always shuffling along behind, him with his hands always up on her shoulders, him always with his hands reaching up out to my mother like that, with his hands up on her shoulders like that, her always looking to me like she was walking him the way you would look if you were walking an imbecile, as if there were something wrong with the man, wrong with the way the man was—but there was nothing wrong with the way my father was—my father just liked to walk like that whenever my father went walking with my mother, and my father never went walking without my mother.

I mean, this is what they did, this is how they did it when I saw them, this is what I saw when I saw my parents get old whenever I went down to Florida and had to see my old parents walk.

Try picturing more minutes.

I think I must have told you that we made it on time.

Only it was not anything like what I had been picturing when I had sat myself down on the airplane and started keeping myself busy picturing the kind of funeral I was going to be seeing when I got down to Florida for the funeral my father was going to have.

Picture this.

It was just a rabbi they had gone ahead and hired.

To my mind, the man was too young-looking and too good-looking. I kept thinking the man probably had me beat in both departments. I kept thinking how much the man was getting paid for this and would it come to more or would it come to less than my ticket down and ticket back.

I felt bigger than I had ever felt.

I did not know where the ashes were. I did not know how the burning was done. There were some things which I knew I did not know.

But I know that I still felt bigger than I had ever felt.

As for him, the rabbi took a position on one side of the room, the rabbi stood himself up on one side of the room, and me and my sister and my mother, we all went over to where we could tell we were supposed to go over to on the other side of the room, some of the time sitting and some of the time standing, but I cannot tell you how it was that we ever knew which one it was meet and right for us to do.

I heard: "Father of life, father of death."

I heard the rabbi say: "Father of life, father of death."

I heard the guy who was driving the limo say, "Get your mother's feet."

Picture us back in the limo again. Picture us stopping off at a delicatessen. Picture me and my mother sitting and waiting while my sister gets out and goes in to make sure they are going to send over exactly what it was we had ordered when she called up and called our order in.

Maybe it would help for you to picture things if I told you that what my mother has on her head is a wig of plastic hair that fits down over almost all of her ears.

It smells in here.

I can smell the smell of them in here.

And of every single one of the sandwiches that just came over from the delicatessen in here.

Now picture it like this—the stuff came hours ago and so far this is all that has come. I mean, the question is this—where are all of the neighbors which this death was supposed to have been ordered for?

I just suddenly realized that you might be interested in finding out what we finally decided on.

The answer is four corned beef on rye, four turkey on rye, three Jarlsberg and lettuce on whole wheat, and two low-salt tuna salad on bagel.

Now double it—because we are figuring strictly a half sandwich apiece.

Here is some more local color.

The quiz programs are going off and the soap operas are coming on and my sister just got up and went to go lie down on my mother's bed and I can tell you that I would go and do the same if I was absolutely positive that it would not be against my religion for me to do it—because who knows what it could be against for you to go lie down on your father's bed?—it could be some kind of a curse on you that for the rest of your life it would keep coming after you until, ha ha, just like him, that's it, you're dead.

My mother says to me, "So tell me, sonny, you think we got reason to be nervous about the coffee?"

My mother says to me, "So what do you think, sonny, you think I should go make some extra coffee?"

My mother says to me, "I want for you to be honest with me, sweetheart, you think we are taking too big of a chance the coffee might not be more than plenty of enough coffee?"

My mother says to me, "So what is it that is your opinion, darling, is it your opinion that we could probably get away with it if your mother does not go put on another pot of coffee?"

Nobody could have pictured that.

Nor have listened to no one calling us and no one imploring us for us to hold everything, for us to keep the coffee hot, that they are right this minute racing up elevators and running down stairways and rushing along corridors and will be any second knocking at the door because there is a new widow in the building and an old man just plotzed.

You know what?

I do not think that you are going to have to picture anything along the lines of any of that.

Except for maybe Mr. Goldbaum.

Here is Mr. Goldbaum.

Mr. Goldbaum is the man who sticks his head in at the door which we left open for the company which was on the way over.

Here is Mr. Goldbaum talking.

"You got an assortment, or is it all fish?"

That was Mr. Goldbaum.

My mother says, "That was Mr. Goldbaum."

My mother says, "The Mr. Goldbaum from the building."

Now you can picture a whole different thing, a whole different place.

This time it's the Sunday afterwards.

So picture this time this—my sister and me the Sunday afterwards. Picture the two different cars we rented to get out from the city to Long Island to the cemetery. Picture the cars parked on different sides of the administration building which we are supposed to meet at for us to meet up with the rabbi who has been hired to say a service over the box which I am carrying of ashes.

Picture someone carrying ashes.

Not because I am the son but because the box is made out of something too heavy.

Now here is a picture you've had practice with.

Me and my sister waiting.

Picture my sister and me standing around where the offices are of the people who run the cemetery, which is a cemetery way out on Long Island in February.

I just suddenly had another thought which I just realized. What if your father was the kind of a father who was dying and he called you to him and he said you were his son and he said for you to come lie down on the bed with him so that he as your father could hold you and so that you as his son could hold him so that the both of you could both be like that hugging each other like that for you to say goodbye to each other before you had to go actually go leave each other and you did it, you did it, you got down on the bed with your father and you got down up close to your father and you got your arms all around your father and your father was hugging you and you were hugging your father and there was one of you who could not stop it, who could not help it, but who just got a hard-on?

Or both did?

Picture that.

Not that I and my father ever hugged like that.

Here comes the next rabbi.

This rabbi is not such a young-looking rabbi, is not such a good-looking rabbi, is a rabbi who just looks like a rabbi who is cold from just coming in like a rabbi from outside with the weather.

The rabbi says to my sister, "You are the daughter of the departed?"

The rabbi says to me, "You are the son of the departed?"

The rabbi says to the box, "These are the mortal remains of the individual which is the deceased party?"

Maybe I should get you to picture the cemetery.

Because this is the cemetery where we all of us are getting buried in—wherever we die, even if in Florida.

I mean, our plot's here.

My family's is.

The rabbi says to us, "As we make our way to the gravesite, I trust that you will want to offer me a word or two about your father so that I might incorporate whatever ideas and thoughts you have into the service your mother called up and ordered, may God give this woman peace."

Okay, picture him and me and my sister all going back outside in February again all over again in February again and I am the only one who cannot get his gloves back on because of the box, because of the canister—because of the motherfucking urn—which is too heavy for me to handle without me holding onto it every single instant with both of my hands.

The hole.

The hole I am going to have to help you with.

The hole they dug up for my father is not what I would ever be able to picture in my mind if somebody came up to me and said to me for me to do my best to picture the hole they make for you when you go see your father's grave.

I mean, the hole was more like the hole you would go dig for somebody if the job they had for you to do was to cover up a big covered dish.

Like for a casserole.

And that is not the half of it.

Because what makes it the half of it is the two cinder blocks which I can see are already down in it when I go to put down the urn down in it, the hole.

And as for the other half?

This is the two workmen who come over from somewhere I

wasn't ready for anybody to come over from and who put down two more cinder blocks on top of what I just put in.

You know what I mean when I say cinder blocks?

I mean those gray blocks of gray cement or of gray concrete that when they refer to them they call them cinder blocks and they've got holes in them for you to grab.

Four of those.

Whereas what I had always thought was that what they did with a grave was fill things back in it with what they took out.

Unless they had taken cinder blocks out.

You can go ahead and relax now.

It is not necessary for you to lend yourself to any further effort to create particularities that I myself was not competent to render.

Except it would be a tremendous help for me if you would do your best to listen for the different sets of bumps the different sets of tires make when we all three of us pass over the little speed bump that makes everybody go slow before coming into and going out of the cemetery my family is in.

Three cars, six sets of tires—that's six bumps, I count six bumps and a total of twenty-six half sandwiches—six sounds of hard cold rubber in February of 1986.

Or hear this—the rabbi's hands as he rubs the wheel to warm the wheel where he has come to have the habit of keeping his grip in place on the wheel when—to steer, to steer—the rabbi puts his hands on the wheel and thinks:

"Jesus shat."

That's it.

I'm finished.

Except to inform you of the fact that I got back to the city not via the Queens Midtown Tunnel but via the Queensboro Bridge since with the bridge you beat the toll, that and the fact that I went right ahead and sat myself down and started trying to picture some of the things which I have just asked you for you to picture for me, that and the fact that I had to fill in for myself where the holes were sometimes too big for anybody to get a good enough picture of them, the point being to get something written, the point being to get anything written, and then get paid for it, to get paid for it as much as I could get paid for it, this to cover the cost of Delta down and Delta back. Avis at their Sunday rate, plus extra for liability and collision.

One last thing—which is that no one told me.

So I just took it for granted that where it was supposed to go was go down in between them.

HUSTLERS ALL IN THE ROGUE-SNOWN NIGHT

Gotta make this fast, which gotta's herein indited because I've got no more than the quickest minute for me to honor Denis Johnson. Am still, and expect to remain so, under the spell of the Johnsonette I just a lick ago read—it's got largesse in its title, which work (not to mention, word), to my mind, one hundred ten percent earns every right to claim, the book the story shows up in just handed me by the daughter—her name is Tracey—of a buddy of mine, whose name was Joan until she switched it a thousand years ago to Jonnie, and who believing me in urgent need of falling in love with something written, what Tracey had just herself fallen in love with (the Johnsonette, I mean, with the word largesse in the title), rushed over me-ward so that my habitual lovelornness, I suppose Tracey and Jonnie deduced, could be interrupted for a little bit. All this in mitten drinnin of my rereading some somber (sombre?) Camus, which particular Camus I'm not telling, got it?—but up to this instant, quit it, the Camus, in order for Tracey to get her book back in her righteous possession right away—and, I swear, my best intention is sworn to going right morosely back to the Camus as soon as I have done this deed à la my saying to you what I want to hear myself say apropos of Johnson's story, what it made me think of, and feel, feel, apart from, yes,

yes, you bet, my falling head over—etc., etc.—in love with it, not to mention Johnson too, as our Tracey must certainly have come to the cunning opinion I would. So here we go or there we went, mitten drinnin, Gordon dropping everything: the Camus, plus the kitchen-waxing supplies I was just that second getting out for me to have a go at restoring to scratch the status of my pride and joy—viz. the sealed—sealed!—terra-cotta kitchen floor tiles, plus the cloths, the utility cloths. I am now, at this not unimpressively advanced stage of life, totally unapologetic about my having declined into a Mop & Glo type, not the old carnauba-wax-famed devotee I used to be well rearward of today's date, this surrender to ease encouraged in my bones not only by age but also thanks to my ex-neighbor, Barbara Fiore (she's passed, she's passed, yeah, yeah, dead), who destroyed my Boeing Brush Master before she fell down on her once–Boeing Brush Master'd kitchen floor, thus doing it, passing, that is. But, swell, that Barbara's dead and my Barbara's, she's dead, and now here's Tracey, Jonnie's daughter, passing the Johnson book into my rubber-gloved hands, and what do I with unforgiving eyes right away see?

I see aulde Denis Johnson's done it too, passed, just up and passed, and before I go giving myself over to any humane act of largesse, let's suppose there was, well, this, let's describe it as, vexed history between Johnson and myself that, from my point of view anyway, was not the genialest (or do I mean congenialest?) of histories. I'd been tossed out on my ear from my post as fiction editor at *Esquire*, the tossing done by two villainous merchants of wrong all of a sudden in charge of me (one Byron Dobell, now deceased; the other, Clay Felker, to name names, ditto, dead), my collection and recollection of exasperations now made rampant by the book in my hand. All this was chiefly, albeit not entirely, absolutely on account of the deduction, abduction, corporate reduction of the swellest boss you could ever in all your imaginings imagine to be bossed by—I mean Harold Hayes, of course, canned before the rascals canned me, Hayes also being the U.S.'s most puckish of editors-in-chief, him too, ditto passed, ditto deceased, from, or is it of, brain cancer, the man, then jobless, dispatched to and therefore, at death, in residency in *California*, of all places, more or less biding time while my longtime buddy William H. Ryan, *Bill!*, also fired from *Esquire*, but in Ryan's case on account of his nearly braining (police called to the scene) then art director, a tremendously stand-up edition of Britness, oh, oh, brave Richard Weigand. But anyway, anyway, anyway, am I losing the thread? Look, wasn't it the unfriendly sense I had à la Johnson, wasn't I preparing myself to explain this to you, getting set to detail it, aulde Gordo hanging at the threshold of the kitchen with the Johnson book in his hand reviewing in *my* soul, my, a thousand years ago, having performed criminally to give this, who he, Denis Johnson, a three-story lift out of the *Esquire* slush pile (a publishing buzzword I want my admirers in Bolivia and Paraguay to know whose objectionable commonality I myself, your good, clean-hearted Gordo, never once indulged in—well, until, oh God, just now, I suppose) the day *after* I'd been sent packing, the day *after* I was officially off my throne, sitting musing on the floor of my office bullshitting with Nora Ephron, smoking whining vowing ineffable manners of death to the usurpers?

Oh boy, now Nora Ephron herself (yeah, yeah, I know, I know, all of the way out of here, kaput)—when, whilst, all deposed, I'm stacking the slush, I glance at some MSS and determine to my satisfaction hey, hey, hey! I believe I will just go ahead and get out three P.O.'s and backdate them three weeks or better, so take that, you off-planet invaders, you order-takers! You sonsofnewesqybitches! Lish strikes again! And off I go, well, am dispossessed, shuttled to, hooray, hooray, Alfred A. Knopf, mere blocks away, head crammed with miseries of Jill Goldstein, who took a header out her office window right onto Madison Avenue, of Ryan in *California* off in the wings for the exhibition of Hayes' consent, he, Bill—*Bill!*—wrenching the wheel a particularly decisive turn leftward, westward, round about Ukiah, off Route One and into the whole damnable Pacific. Anyway, I am, to come to today, an inch shy of making a begrudging swipe at a half-hearted launch of my distracted attention (I was ankle-deep into some Camus, you might recall my telling you). Let's, for the sake of the poetry of it, say I'm thinking "largesse," is it, eh? Johnson's soliciting largesse from *me*? Is this not the same bastard who had all the opportunity in the world to say thanks for cheating for me, Gordo? Is, or is this not, the bastard who'd greeted me with a fingertipping when he'd sight of DeLillo's sitting in the seat beside me at some Will Eno thing? Is this not the bastardo about whom I'd leaned to DeLillo and asked who was that guy who was just here, some hustler, you know?

And DeLillo must have said Denis Johnson, okay?

And I: "Well, talk about a hustler who works a room."

Did DeLillo say, "You're not? You don't?"

Nope, DeLillo didn't say any such, but who's to prove he didn't think it?

So, reader, reader, I just want you to know I am in a very unlargessical mood recalling the foregoing, you know? But, whoa, Jesus Christ, I stand there with my tool belt there at the threshold noting Jesus Christ, dead dead dead too?—and choking with lamentation and yet to be overtaken by gratitude, I read—and am slaughtered by the beauty.

Slaughtered!

Good God, what a guy!

The splendor of this writing!

Especially, I hasten to admit, because there's in it, in the "largesse" bit, a passage that hurtles up at me off the page and seizes me with the grip only a consort of my private kishkes could exert.

It must be, it must have been, sometime before 1984 because in 1984 I took the pledge—but am already blotto, yes, yes, am thoroughly out of my gourd, hopelessly stranded leagues from my tree, horribly desanguinated from the little left of blood in me in the one teensy vein left upstairs—this at a veddy veddy Park Avenue book party, a fancy-dress sit-down affair, of all unbearable things, and I am minus Barbara because Barbara rarely had the forbearance for such goings-on, and I was—*am*—sitting with on one side of me my agent, Lynn Nesbit (pal of Barbara's more or less owing to their shared Midwestern debuts), observer of all that I will do and say (all of which will be reported back to Barbara on the morrow, mmm?), and on the other side of me there sits a woman resolved to make herself as pixilated as ever anybody could, so since Nesbit's nice and all but not a mysterious stranger, I rounds on the mysterious stranger, in the certainty that she longs to be entertained by examples from my Shmulevitz repertoire.

So I says to her Shmulevitz is mooching around on the thoroughfare and espies this young thing mooching around qua and he sidles up to her and says to her what are you doing loitering on this corner, because I am a whore she says and this is my corner, prompting Shmulevitz to say so what do you get, whereupon she says I get by way of gelt twenty-eight dollars and thirty-five cents, to which Shmulevitz says in reply what do you say to nineteen dollars and fifty cents, the answer to which is at that price I wouldn't even be breaking even.

Reader, reader, you tell me how this, what you just heard, is construed as a prelude that leads to an interlude. The mysterious stranger laughs and laughs and we grab each other in high hilarity, rush from the table (not even a shrewd adieu to Nesbit), and it is maybe not yet five in the morning that I awake all of the way up in the sky in a Park Avenue building one building away, to the north, to the south, in terror.

I cannot find the major components of my dinner clothes and accessories.

I can find but one glossy shoe.

I cannot find the door out.

I land in the lobby blind from the glare of marble, both the doormen on duty lurching at me to steady me in my lurch, to defend the statuary, to protect the palace codes, to turn up the blare of the ducats robbed from Fifth Avenue and on round-the-clock covertly manipulated display.

Over the roar, or was it under it, of a cataract of cortical fluid draining from miles overhead, I hear, "Sir, may we call a cab for you, sir?"

Once a wrangler-in-training at a dude ranch on an Arizona plateau, parallel to a butte, embedded deep in an arroyo, I wave off this intelligent intercession, take ingenious aim, adjust for windage and steerage and roil, and fling myself out of range of the uniformed paracletes, is the word, and into the strange nocturne beyond.

Reader, reader, you must tarry with the Johnson fiction.

It's real, I'm sure.

As was what befell myself.

For I have come to a stop, am of the belief that I am now standing sockless, no more than one patent leather shoe to the good, grappling my person at an approach to the diagonal by virtue of the anchorage offered me by my having taken hold of two-thirds of a pant leg and both wings of a clip-on bow tie.

But am alive, alive, standing, standing, at a bias, or is it on one?—in at least a half foot of new-blown snow.

On Park Avenue.

What's this?

What did I see?

Have the heavens, whilst I dallied, let fly with some very un-Shmulevitzy joke?

Has it, I ask you, snown?

It is night.

It is snow, snow, snow.

In the riverine bassoonist wilderness up and down the famous avenue.

Thirty-seven blocks from home.

Cab?

There was no cab, no taxi, no nothing in sight, even in the distance there was not a merciful Gulliver of a pedestrian to take me on his back.

There was nothing transportative anywhere.

It was all just that sheen, an empty and hushed ex-urbanity—and I was the screwball fool, drunk, shameless, all undone, thirty-seven blocks from—well, you heard.

The only transport I dare propose to you, as Denis Johnson rehabilitatively does for his principal figure in the terrific "The Largesse of the Sea Maiden," is that which arose in me as I beheld, on Park Avenue, an ordinary accidental glory.

A vision of snow.

A gotcha downfall of it not impossibly signifying the fallenness of your condition—that once-in-a-life look you maybe might get of the superb universe from where you wobble in sin and shame and folly, all three.

On Park Avenue no less.

A snowblast of gotcha timing and proportion.

It was so wonderful.

There was no disaster, no catastrophe, no undoing of all I held dear—at home, in truth, in the world.

O where fled the dread and the petty when the undeserved bounty came and showed itself to the mad?

No fear, no fright, no anguish, no kidding.

Just the unction of the unbidden snow.

I was insane—and insanely happy.

This, for a fleetsome instant, pal, was deliverance.

Man oh man, in Johnson's case. I bet it really happened to the bastard, his once ducking indoors to get out of the weather, taking his place up on a stool in some Park Avenue bistro, thence (Christ, I'm not even exactly positive what thence means, am I?), but, anyhow, yeah, thence welcomed to an audience with the keeper of the cure.

Bewitchment granted—consolation—for me snowfall, for Johnson a sea maiden—on the Upper East Side of Manhattan.

Thank you, Denis Johnson.

Thank you, Jonnie Greene and Tracey Riese.

Thank you, one and all, for the difference, distinction, invention of your hustles.

Hell, this is just Ninety-Sixth Street and it's early late August while outside—oh, damn it, man—outside there's still the bad bug killing what it can—but, hey, admit it, aren't there meshugenah times when life is just too great for words?

Fine, fine—now there's the Camus for me to open back up again, to finish what was started—Camus's plodding reconnoiter with the grim involution of things in grisly general, as they otherwise irreparably, unimprovably, all-too-humanly, altogether naturally, are.

The facts.

The chore to be done in the kitchen, then the rags to be washed or discarded, then the bottle of Mop & Glo to be stashed back in the laundry room cabinet, the fucking forever hassle of hassling the tricky Mop & Glo's ruthlessly twisty spout back onto how it belongs to be, closed and preserved from leakage—until the next goddamn slog on old hands and older knees—then supper, then scuffing up the tiles again, then pills to sleep, the touch of bed linen rather more abrasion than caress—no, no reconstitution by reason of any Park Avenue hideaway apparition appearing hauntingly in the real desolation likely to visit me as a personal panorama of loony abandon, of perfection, rebirth, renewal, flurries of sweet howdies to you, Gordo, crooned, schemed, ordained just for you, Gordo, accruing to you in the crowded corners of your dreams.

JAMIE GILLIS, HIS LETTER

I was, not for many years but for very many moments, terribly happy in the company of a fellow named Jamie Gillis. If you know enough about fuck films, chances are you might know something about Gillis. He got his living performing in fuck films, a career he told me he had made his way into on the strength of a recommendation offered him by Martin Scorsese when the men met at Columbia University. I cannot remember any further detail to do with Gillis scoring his first job, only that the two men were said, by Gillis, to have met in the course of something to do with moviemaking. Or perhaps it was N.Y.U. My memory's wreckage.

At any rate, Christmas days away in 2009, the letter carrier brought to my door the letter that follows. The letter following that letter is the letter I produced (that would be the word, wouldn't it?) the night I had returned home—early, as it was—from the Christmas eve party Gillis gave at the little wood house he occupied in Midtown. Or is it Eve? The name Gillis my friend Jamie told me he took from the woman he had been nursing during her slow surrender to cancer. I also nursed a woman for many years. She was my wife Barbara, overcome by motor neuron disease, dead at sixty-four pounds. This tells you something of what's ahead. No, no, it doesn't.

The two letters, Jamie's to me, my reply to him, were placed in a single envelope that has rested tilted against the wall back behind this typewriter ever since. Jamie's aim was to put me on notice *before the party*; my floral reply, *after the party*, was to enforce the view which of us was the one who could put syntax where plain speech ought to have been. Gillis died not long afterward. The Watson referred to is James D. Watson. That one, yes—my letter adverting to the day we spent out in Cold Spring Harbor being taken about by the director of the lab for us to marvel at the latest in the way of construction. All clear now? Oh, always, everything—everything is always all too clear.

At the party? At the party I kept myself busy trying to keep out of everyone's way, especially that of the condemned man. I recall saying hello to Penn and Teller, Gilbert Gottfried, Kathleen Turner. Stayed, in all, well less than an hour. Grabbed a big shrimp on my way out up from very near the bottom of a big colorful bowl that sat enormously halfway along on the long table that stood mid-floor before you could get to the door that led you up two steps out of the subterranean kitchen sinking deeper into the city under the burden of such a bounty of exotic foodstuffs and sad jolly people. Spit the mangled shrimp back into my hand and put my hand into one of the big side pockets of my big-pocketed canvas coat. Too spicy for me, too sassy, too acrimonious by far for me to manage. Dropped the mess I'd made on the sidewalk when I'd gotten myself back out into the terrific cold and promptly ducked down enough for me to see if I could see back into the kitchen and saw, for my bother, my friend for the last time before walking the fifty blocks to go to get home. Did I see Jamie Gillis laughing or crying when I saw him bent over or sagging against the long table where the shrimp bowl had been positioned for the revelers to reach in? Couldn't tell. Will never know. Got home and sat down in front of this exhausted Underwood and typed the letter that put posing where an act of meaning should have gone. You'll see this after you see Jamie Gillis's handwritten declaration to me. No, I'm certain of it, you won't miss a thing. Does anyone ever?

12/21/09

MY VERY DEAR GORDON,
    I AM WRITING IN PRINT BLOCKS TO MAKE THIS A
LITTLE EASIER TO DECIPHER.
    ENJOYING MUCH YOUR 8 LAST GIFTS (AND TRUE GIFTS
THEY ARE) "MY ROMANCE" AND "ARCADE". PERHAPS BECAUSE
I KNOW THERE WILL BE NO MORE TO COME, ~~I AM~~ THESE
LAST 2 SEEM TO RESONATE WITH ME EVEN MORE THAN
~~YOUR~~ EARLIER GIFTS ~~OF~~ FROM YOUR SAINTLY SELF.
    BUT ENOUGH ABOUT YOU.

Ho! Ho! Ho!
BUT SERIOUSLY
FOLKS.

    YOU'RE GONNA LAUGH, BUT I'M DYING.
IT'S NO JOKE, NO SHIT, NO FOOLIN'.
    I TELL YOU THIS NOW SO YOU WILL NOT ~~FEEL~~ FEEL
AWKWARD OR EMBARRASSED ON XMAS EVE IF YOU
HAPPEN TO NOTICE MY LOSS OF ~~WEIGHT~~ WEIGHT, OR THE
FACT THAT I NOW TEND TO LIMP A BIT.
    YOU WILL BE AMONG THE COOL, HIP, IN CROWD
OF FAMILY & FRIENDS WHO ARE AWARE OF MY
CONDITION (A RARE, UNTREATABLE LITTLE THING
CALLED MUCOSAL MELANOMA) AND WILL NOT MAKE
A BIG DEAL ABOUT IT. OF COURSE YOU ARE FREE
TO CRY AND TOTALLY BREAK DOWN OVER THIS NEWS
AT YOUR LEISURE AT HOME.
    I AM, GENERALLY SPEAKING, STILL IN GOOD SPIRITS
AND REALIZE IT WOULD BE THE HEIGHT OF INGRATITUDE
TO BEMOAN MY FATE NOW, AFTER HAVING LIVED
SUCH A BLESSED ~~AND~~ LIFE.
    PLEASE CALL TO LET ME KNOW YOU HAVE RECEIVED
THIS LETTER BEFORE XMAS EVE. IF YOU DON'T DO THAT I
WILL CALL YOU TO GIVE YOU THIS LATEST JUICY BIT OF GOSSIP.
        LOOKING FORWARD TO SEEING MY
        GREAT AND GRAND AMIGO
                    646 334 46

Christmas Eve, 2009

My friend,

Let us be nursed as we ourselves have nursed. As we found, it
was the only balm--touch, touch, touch. How wondrous, this
solitary gift, far more to effect than even the touching that the
eyes can do. Words, feh!--they in course prove only a bother,
all too customarily offered, all too excruciatingly heard
struggling under the blemish the tarnish of use accumulates.
Touch, it seems to me, exceeds all else, and so, from this
distance, I reach for you and touch you, a comfort, please find,
truer than love.

Your friend,

P. S. Turned up one of Watson's nails from our tour of the lab.
Had taken it from the construction site we were strolling around
for such a tedious while in. Stuck it in a pocket of the much-
waxed jacket you so kindly noticed: a crazy memento that came
back up out of the pocket and into my hand a few days ago when
the weather had made itself cold enough for me to risk the wear
and tear to be done to my prized, most-stewarded garment. The
big nasty thing--a spike, really--came up out of the pertinent
pocket and into my fingers--and with it the startlement not of
memory but of the ritornello of very life leisurely reliving
itself: everything, everyone, the unfinished grandiosity of the
building, all of it all over again and forever again, in less
than--look, just look!--an instant.

JUNE THIRTY-FOURTH

Or, of course, the thirty-fourth of June, if you will, mmm? Suit yourself. Deign it as you wish it. As for yours very truly, I am thoroughly unequal to the deciding of the matter. Not that I for a nonce am possessed of the sentiment that the matter brought before us (to wit: June thirty-fourth, this version, versus the thirty-fourth of June, that one) fails to matter much.

May I be granted leave to say what is without matter?

In an experience constituted of the sidelong, in a world constituted of the quantical, in a cosmos constituted of a proportionate complement of the unseen and perhaps the unseeable, what can be said to be matterless?

Or without matter?

Or apart from mattering?

Or of no matter at all—none, none, none?

Hence, the exasperations of determining the expression of the date cited, indecisively, to be sure, above. Not that the family dog, who now answers to the name, you may as well be promptly told, Vincent, however wedded the hound was to the appellation Louise when fetched through the basement door to us for to commence inhabiting the premises with Penelope and me, appears to care.

She, Penelope herself, partook herself of one look at the animal and pronounced her to be designated thereafter as is now known.

Vincent.

She abides among us without noticeable complaint.

So much for the principal features of the household, albeit I might offer the observation that there is in it with us, up to its neck, a grandmother clock whose station has, for the duration of an era, been lodged here in the posture of an upright stance yet at sufficient of a tilt for it to lean itself against an eastward-facing section of wall in the pleasantest of living rooms, and, moreover, whose tolling (that is the grandmother clock, yes?) of the hour perdured, insofar as we may swear in pledgement our honor and fortune, altogether quite properly—up until the trio of the parties accounted for succumbed to slumber and thus to states of reduced consciousness precluding the bearing of honest witness to the contrary, howsoever sleep-vexed attention proved expectably averted to an anticipation of the dawn's disclosure of a calendric progress to June thirty-fifth, save you say, for the sake of your druthers, the thirty-fifth of June.

Are we clear?

Are we, despite fathomless differences baked into the cake, joined in our adventure into the mad, the berserk, the everyday mishegas of the housebound?

Look, just to steady ourselves and vouchsafe synchrony, I put it to you that Jack Sprat could eat no fat, his wife could eat no lean, and that such it was betwixt themselves they licked the platter clean.

It's Vincent's go-to bedtime fave.

That and "Lullaby and Goodnight," and so on and so forth, it being Penelope who, between us, can croon it to its finito, and it is I who, haplessly, am already (by then) asleep, this when we three have consented to call it quits for the day and to repair to our appointed places to allow the night to pass, Pen (a convenience, mmm?) having blanched, lashings of olive oil and snipped garlic into the bargain, Swiss chard, a repast prepared in such surplusage as to furnish Vin's plate (what's not habit-forming, *nes pah?*) with more than ample in the way of savor and nutrition, allotments all salted and peppered to taste.

You now have before you the highlights of the matter in question.

A day like any angry other—except for the exception noted.

June et cetera et cetera went forward as, hitherto, unfurled. So it now remains for me to list words I know but which, in a seizure of certitude, I deemed that they be kept out of the composition thitherto presented.

All set?

Here goes.

Gusset, Flume, Tendrilous, Hectograph, Throbble, Triune, Lissome, Ribaldry, Equanimous, Riggish, Carceral, Vernissage, Demimondaine, Gulosity, Raillery, Inanition, Placatory, Barulum, Aporia, Saccadic, Thirled, Screak, Qubit, Mystagogue, Percipium, Gawe, Shtum, Churring, Frictive, Concitation, Precarity, Thetic, Lustration, Proleosis, Catachresis, Shambolic, Stochastic, Kraken, Hammam, Anoesis, and Fossick.

And hereafter find my prospective itinerary for 2021.

Leatherhead, North Stoke, Clewer, Lowestoft, and Rotherhithe.

Oh, I might remark Mother—Regina, Reggie, Reg, Regeleh—often said of herself, when she had taken pains to adorn her person for an event involving socializing, that she was gussied-up, and, furthermore, it was plain for one to see that Mother's oftenest partner at mah-jongg was a woman who went by the name Gussie.

Curiously, interestingly, even intriguingly, my father's best friend's given name was Gustave, which fellow—Gustave, that is—was invariably addressed as Gus, and who was never, in my ken, referred to as other than thus.

Just mentionably, there was a good deal of napping on June the thirty-fourth, unless it be that the thirty-fourth of June has managed to enjoy top billing in your preferments. With regard to the day after the day of wrath, and, in all geniality, to the matter of how the succeeding day was dealt with by the date-stewarding devices held by the household as authoritative informants, can't say.

Slept through it.

Pen and Vin?

Per usual, neither's talking.

WATCH OUT!

At all events, I aim to enumerate the "curiosities" that piled up yesterday, and will then shut up.

Or was it today?

Who knows?

What does WHEN matter?

First, it's well before dawn, probably around when we had first taken to bed for the night (we are in the practice of retiring very late, being big fans of the program *Dateline*, dozens of which we have recorded, both of us mad for Keith Morrison, one of the three emcees, a striking, high-sneakered—often, if the shot shows his footwear—guy from Saskatchewan, as in our neighbor to the north, a province or something, canton, parish, I don't know, where I once taught for a week, farming country, very affecting).

Anyway, well before sun-up, the phone rings, scaring us both to death. Who is it? It's not some scam call but a guy whom I have not spoken to since my late teens, guy named Eric, and it's no bullshit, none, because I immediately recognize the voice, even after all the years, my being eighty-six as of now, and I say, words to this effect, Jesus, Eric (a name I do not particularly care for), it's you, man, what's up, for pity's sake, how on earth did you get this number, is there an emergency, what, what? And he tells me

his missus has crapped out and he's feeling pretty in need of company, can he pick up some sandwiches, which would I like, with
mayo or not, and I say hey, I'm sorry to hear about your wife but
mine is right here sleeping and she has tremendous obligations in
the workday almost every day and we're not exactly social people
in the first place and there is the lockdown, don't you know, and
we've both been sheltering in place since February and, honestly,
we eat just the one meal a day, and Jesus, man, hey, Eric, where do
you live anyway, and he says Rockville, Maryland, and I say shit,
Rockville, that's the town a former student of mine from the fifties
owns half of, I hear, his labs and all, Craig Venter, you know him
or of him, from TV and everywhere, ever hear of J. Craig Venter, the wizard of Rockville and La Jolla? And Eric says no, I just
thought, you know, so okay, it's cool, thanks, sorry to wake you,
guess I'll just call Butch or Chet, and I say shit, Eric, hey, man,
that's a long drive from Rockville, and my wife has imposed a no-
sandwich rule, and I'm just so sorry as all get-out for your grief and
all and please accept my tenderest condolences, maybe some time
when all this is over, if it ever will be, maybe you can come on up
and we'll grab some lunch in my neighborhood, there's this coffee
shop almost next door and, true, the staff's a bit on the crabby side
but, hey, they've got terrific fries and fried chicken, no, you know
what we'll do, E-guy, you know what we'll do, you've got a car,
right?—where he interrupts me, half sobbing, says no, he does not
have transportation, and I say big deal, entirely unnecessary, the
buses and subways here will see us to the good if they're operating,
but come on, man, it's sort of a big family secret but Penelope,
that's my wife and all, both Frances and Barbie died—years ago,
my God, but look, you take the train up and we'll make a real
thing of it and go to what Pen and I happen to believe is the best
fried chicken joint in America, no shit, Eric, this outfit, it's called

Bobwhite, just a hole in the wall, pal, but you won't believe it, all the way downtown and all the way east and you have to squeeze in the door, E-man, you listening, it's called Bobwhite and you never, I promise you, have been in the company of fried chicken to equal it, and just because you are my good old pal and happen to be in deep need of consolation and condolence and treats, I am going to tell you the secret name of it, it's Bobwhite, which I may have already told you but you can't be too careful, Bobwhite, no sign outside, just a mob inside—E-guy, you got something to note this down with, and he says yeah, but real sad-like, very downbeat, and I say Eric, pal, hey, E-man, cheer up, buddy, be of good cheer, it's called Bobwhite and it's way off the beaten track and you will be one of the few lucky people to ever get a shot at it, way east, I grant you, very way east, and there's some walking involved, sure, but you have never had the like, guaranteed, fried chicken for the gods, nothing to match it, it's the cure, man, the fucking cure, E-man, and no big bite on a man's purse, and it's on me anyway, like when is this, it's what, what, I mean, it's now what, what month, it's August, right, so like in December, let's figure, you come up, we'll hook up at Grand Central, you'll meet Pen, she's a knockout, Pen is, I mean she's some looker, E-man, and funny, she's a living scream, a riot, you never heard such wit from a human being who's hardly in long pants yet, and so figure December maybe—which is when I realize he is no longer on the line, has hung up or been disconnected and I go right back to sleep, say nothing to Pen, what's the diff, but then what, it comes time for me be awake, the phone call, the depression, this guy, Eric whatever, I'm awake, I'm awake, I can't get back to sleep, so I make my way into the living room, having first tried to take a leak and, as some guys know all too enragingly well, prostate, prostate, can't piss, sit there for maybe five minutes trying to read and go, or reread for the fifth time DeLillo's *Players*, and no, I can't go, sleeping pills still got me unresponsive down there, and I am just lifting my undies and what do I see where the book is open, I see, on the flyleaf I think it's called or no, it's something else, some other official part of a book, I see this, in my handwriting, indubitably, fucking indubitably it's my handwriting, but from years back, God knows how many, which I can tell from the quality of the scribble, that's me, all right, but back in the eighties, or seventies, or whenever *Players* came out, I see that I have written, oh, I wish you could see it, I wish I could show it to you, it is so creepy, so, at least for me and probably for Pen, but this was long before Penny was even born, for pity sake, or pity's sake, but there, in the front of the book, never descried before, never spotted, not once come across, up at the top of the page and coming down it about a quarter page, to a depth like that deep, this: *Most sons must be summoned as I was. Come now. Hurry. Esophagus worse. They meant my father's esophagus. My mother does crossword puzzles.* That, my friend, is it. That's it.

Christ, how weird!

It's left me jumping out of my skin.

So I show Penny over coffee, but she just shrugs, says so what? Me, I am devastated, really creeped out, upset, feeling strange, you know, but the next minute I get up from our fressatorium to go to the living room, having been so off my feed that I've forgotten to wind the clock, as I have done untold times, and right, I go ahead and lift off the top section, the framed glass part, glassed on all three sides, with the back exposed, and I bend, right?—to rest the thing down atop this rather large, certainly accommodatingly large Russian brass pot, this big shaped thing shaped a shape that neither Pen nor I knows the word for, although I used to know it, I know, so I phone my son and I say Eth, because I am nervous, noting forgetfulness, thinking Jesus senile, am I dotty or potty or what, and I know Ethan has a pile of the stuff, this Russian brass stuff from the Tsarist days, and I ask him, I describe it et cetera, but he has no idea what I'm talking about and *as I am talking the fucking thing* falls, tips off onto the floor, and I say sorry, Eth, forget the call, speak to you anon, and ring off, and am out of my fucking *mind*, the panels of glass are all of them cracked, and I cannot tell you how often Pen has warned me, said don't do it, rest it on the floor, it's nuts for you to try to balance it on top of that pot, whatever it is properly in antiquities talk called, and I just fucking busted it because I guess of distraction, phoning and not concentrating et cetera et cetera, but did Ethan even know what I was getting at, and meanwhile, what—I've produced by inattention and feeling freaky from this and that, I have broken a treasure, a *treasure*.

Jesus, Pen will positively shit a brick. It's wrecked, I've wrecked it, and where do you go to get it set to rights, where to go to get the glass, *antique glass* from maybe the eighteenth century, there is no going out to get anything fixed, do I need to repeat that, *there is no going out to get anything fixed*, so I'm going into the fressatorium to confess, and my guess was right, Pen is shitting a brick, I told you so, I told you so, but at least I checked the time against the watch I keep in the toilet, and fuck, fuck, I can't believe it, it's that fucking E-guy and the inexplicable inscription and the thing outside, must I say it again, the thing outside, and I go back from confessing to go pick up the pieces and am bending way over, and shit, shit, shit! I can hear Penny weeping, and am not sure is that her playacting weeping or real weeping, because she's one out of a million at faking, acting, kidding, you name it, and I am bending over not believing what a shmegeggy I am and blaming not having been able to urinate yet and am doing my best not to get cut in the broken glass and afraid to check on Pen to see if this is just play-weeping I'm hearing and be careful, Gordo, do not cut yourself on what is probably really seventeenth-century Czar or Tsar glass, and get a Russian infection and, Jesus fuck, my eyeglasses fall off, my reading glasses, because otherwise I'd never see the time on the wristwatch with my distance glasses on, and I have just busted irreplaceable shit, and every morning hereafter, or thereafter, I am going to have to look at that top part of the clock and see *the error of my ways*, SEE EVIDENCE EVERY DAY OF WHAT A DUMB CLUCK I am for not doing as cautioned by Pen, not just taking off the top of the clock and letting it rest on the floor but instead balancing it on the top of the pot and talking on the phone POINTLESSLY *at the same time to see if Ethan knows the name I should have known the name of, that shape, that configuration*, and there are my reading glasses on the floor among the smithereens and I step on them, I, Gordo, have stepped on my only pair of reading glasses and there is no reading without them, I am fucked, fucked, I have broken off the sidepiece which in my day was the temple and that was that, and I know from *past experience* when you break off that thing, you kiss it all goodbye, there is no way the optician is going to tell you he can fix it, it's officially fucked and I did it, the temple I have in my hand and what do I think I am now going to do with it, go out to an optician, go to the eyeglass shop, of which type of commerce there are four, count them, four in this neighborhood, et cetera et cetera, and besides, they're unfixable, it's unfixable, goodbye Charley, when has there ever been one of those outfits that's said to you calm calm be calm, mister, we will just take this little screw here and this little tiny screwdriver over here and why why why is it people are always saying little tiny, isn't one of them enough, if it's little, it's tiny, no?

Oh God.

I cannot sit here on this absurd stool in the august presence of the stately Underwood and begin to find my way around the keyboard without my *reading glasses*. I cannot get to first base among these keys without my fucking busted *reading glasses*. But Pen comes into the living room (did she hear me shriek?) and says calm calm calm, be of good cheer, this is no calamity, despite it being clear there is no optometry outfit that's not going to be, please forgive the expression, shuttered, forget it, no eyeglass shop will be open on a bet with *what's going on out there no matter how much of our savings will be sucked up and handed right straight to the devil for a new pair of frames*. Oh, baby, irreplaceable, everything is irreplaceable and the guy wanted to know if I wanted, or if we wanted, mayo on the sandwiches he was going to walk all of the way from Maryland for him to bring here because he's lonely, baby, lonely. Mayo! And Pen says you adore mayonnaise, you're mad for mayonnaise, you can't live without mayonnaise, what a sweet guy that E-guy is, walking all of the way up here from Maryland, and she takes the fucked-up eyeglasses and goes to the utility cabinet in the back of the place and takes down duct tape and goes methodically and ingeniously to work fashioning this jerry-rigged backup for me, saying that's right, that's right, calm calm calm, please be calm, she counsels, all will be well.

Did I tell you, have I told you, we have not ventured out since February? Well, we have neither of us ventured out, been outdoors, OUT OF DOORS, since February. Have not had one foot one inch over either threshold, not since February and it's almost September now? And while the repair work is underway, while I am watching my astonishing wife perform an astonishing feat, the phone rings, *the phone rings!*, which is in itself a miraculous occurrence in this household, and I think oh Jesus is it my old E-pal again with a menu of sandwich options and a day in December all

picked out and word that he is allergic to fried chicken but roast
chicken is okay and I take the receiver off the hook and put it to
my good ear and hear a woman say NOT LOUISE, DO NOT CALL THE
DOG LOUISE, APPLY THE NAME VINCENT INSTEAD and I am about to
faint and I attempt to disconnect but for some reason, on account
of some twilight zone arcanum, I now have a man's voice on the
phone in my ear and I am listening to him while I am still reeling
terrified from the Louise-Vincent thing, the dog thing, I who have
had a dog named Paco and I who have loved no dog more than
I loved Paco, and I think this must be colleagues of Pen's because
Pen, when a kid, battened on evil vicious middle-school pranks
which she would pull on middle-school people and here she is
rigging up useable specs for me while old middle-school confeder-
ates of hers are futzing with the phone in the middle of AN EMER-
GENCY, I have in me this deep hunch, A DESPERATE FORAY INTO
DEEP MEDITATION OF DISCOVERY, which gives me to give her a
half-smile for my catching her at this PERFIDY and LOW-DOWNESS
that the woman and the guy now on the phone are allies of hers
gaslighting me and I'm smiling conspiratorially like I am in on
the gag and the guy is saying bringing me to an unheard-of level
of panic *have you checked your pendulums, have you checked your
pendulums*, HAVE YOU CHECKED YOUR PENDULUMS, and of course
of course of course, as you certainly cannot but have gathered at,
or is it by, this stage of the game there is but one pendulum on
set, as they nowadays have begun saying at every opportunity for
them to sound as if they're hip and in the biz, and anyhow what
the fuck, WHAT THE FUCK, this is no prankster, this is no inside
job, these are no outside jobbers, this is pure craziness, this is all-
night TV shit, this is dial nine one one shit, this is time to call in
the government shit, the outside is now inside, did you hear me,
in that instant I, Gordo, have only one plausible theory, there was

a click somewhere, a switch in the world, a click was clicked and
now *the outside is inside* and we are fucking finished, ruined, wack-
os, or or or all this stuff is a sign, did you hear me, all of these occurrences are illuminations, warnings, emanations, instructions,
commands, the collateral damage of WRITING TOO MUCH, *what
becomes of you when you have overdone it and overwritten!*

The gremlins are inside.

The purgation is underway.

The siege has begun.

In moments from this instant you are going to be very very
SORRY.

I put the receiver back on its cradle, or in it, very very gently
and cautiously and paranoi—skip it, who wants at this juncture
to spell?

I take the "eyeglasses" from Pen with utmost nonchalance. I
sit here, preparing to prepare myself for reparation.

Escape.

A way out for me and my beloved.

A GESTURE FORMING IN MY FOREBRAIN FOR THE INVOCATORY
PRELIM FOR A VERY SEDATE, HARDLY VISIBLE SIGNAL, A WELCOME
TO THE THRESHOLD OF SANCTUARY, REMISSION, A DEAL, NEGOTI-
ATED SETTLEMENT.

I hear, as a resounding one of those famous resonations people
seem so at ease with: "Call that dog Vincent, not Louise."

"Check your pendulums."

Holy God, I nearly pass out.

In fact, I think I did pass out a little bit.

And then I see that my reading glasses, the eyeglasses I need
for when I am seated here at the Underwood ready for action,
are sort of restored, Pen behind me duct-taping her best effort,
achievement, ingenuity to my skull. I, the putz, who leaned over

the mess I made so excessively that my once sweetly submissive spectacles get themselves tipped off my face and *stepped on*, so excessively as to tip the eyeglasses off my face, *stepped on and broken off at the temple*, if that's what you call the pieces on the sides that hook over your ears, and so now I, Gordo, am seated here to play ball with the phantoms in charge, MAKE AMENDS, get the word out to the Dzanc people that I have had it, *that it's too perilous*, ipso facto and words to this effect, that I can foresee that for Penny to get these substitutes off she is going to have to scissor them off day after day, night after night, nap after nap, until I am made hairless and more hideous, they are already, before I even hunt and peck for the first letter, pulling at my eyebrows, it's hopeless and kind of seriously painful, each key an agony, good intentions are nowhere satisfactory ever! This is already impossible—if I want to lie down and try to doze, it cannot be done, IT CANNOT BE DONE without surgery, without MORE THAN I CAN BEAR, *without more cost to what shards remain of me* THAN THIS PRATTLE IS WORTH.

But wait!

The phone again.

A man who says his name is Mr. Whitt or something, phoning from Minnesota or something, saying he wants to know what can I tell him about Peter Christopher and I say who is this and he says that name like Whitt or Witt or Wiz again and that he wishes to consult with me respecting PETER CHRISTOPHER because he, the caller, Mr. Vit maybe, has permission from the widow to proceed with his intention to bring out a reprint of Peter Christopher's collection of stories, *Campfires of the Dead*.

Oh boy.

Old pal, you cannot imagine.

YOU SIMPLY CAN'T.

Wow!

Holy cow!

I say, "His real name was Maroni and he used the name Christopher when he was signing up for my class at Columbia because he was just back out of Nam and owed money to Columbia and figured he could maybe get back in under this other name which so outrageously ill-suited him it was like a curse, a bad omen, a misfit that crushed him to death and was that what killed Peter Maroni or the three kinds of cancer from being a soldier?" I'm sitting on this stool with Pen working to keep the specs from falling off and, my friend, I am thinking that sweetheart of a guy, dead how long ago, a living angel the phantoms would not let live, Peter Maroni alive again via Mr. Vit or Wig—I am so blind and so deaf and so glad.

Campfires of the Dead.

Oh, there is definitely a God.

And so forth.

This God is watching with an eye out of commission but is nevertheless, unless it is nonetheless, catching occasional glimpses of my cousin Peter bicycling in food and supplies for Pen and me, God glancing if not staring at Krupp stuck in Florida and at my buddy Jason Schwartz, also a step from the Floridian abyss, and at Patty and Ryder and Don and at the two Georges and the two Marias and Beth Hawthorne and Jonnie Greene and Margie and Smitty and Paumgarten and the Drs. Mahon and Ethan and his bunk and Sam and Noy and Phoebe and Benjamin Reno and Will and Al and Lutz, Lutz, Lutz, and the Riese family and McCarthy and Hechinger and Fred and Sarah and Fogarty and Kadish and Mohsen and Waldeck and Bobby and Max and the Hogans, the Hogans, and Lorenzo and Jimmy Judge and Mr. Cottrell and Trakas and Ozick and Lobis and Keith Morrison and Mrs. Morrison and Maria Bamford and Maria Bamford's mother and Maria

Bamford's father and Maria Bamford's sister and all the folks in Duluth, or is it spelt Deluth?

And I say hey are we having sesame noodles for dinner tonight and guess who says no we're having stuffed peppers for dinner tonight and I say is there any concoction I cannot abide more than I cannot abide stuffed peppers and she says be glad you got what to eat and I ups to her and says to her can't you tell you're pulling my hair and she ups to me and she says to me who hair, what hair, where hair, and I guess I am now tearing up now for real a little and then tearing up a little more, then now for real a little more NOW because on account of the fact that there is nothing in this life that I cannot handle like Captain Fiction in this life except stuffed peppers.

THE DEATH OF ME

I wanted to be amazing. I wanted to be so amazing. I had already been amazing up to a certain point. But I was tired of being at that point. I wanted to go past that point. I wanted to be more amazing than I had been up to that point. I wanted to do something which went beyond that point and which went beyond every other point and which people would look at and say that this was something which went beyond all other points and which no other boy would ever be able to go beyond, that I was the only boy who could, that I was the only one.

I was going to a day camp which was called the Peninsula Athletes Day Camp and which at the end of the summer had an all-campers, all-parents, all-sports field day which was made up of five different field events, and all of the campers had to take part in all five of all of the different field events, and I was the winner in all five of the five different field events, I was the winner in every single field event, I came in first place in every one of the five different field events—so that the head of the camp and the camp counselors and the other campers and the other mothers and the other fathers and my mother and my father all saw that I was the best camper in the Peninsula Athletes Day Camp, the best in the short run and the best in the long run and the best in the high jump and the best in the broad jump and the best in the event which the Peninsula Athletes Day Camp called the ball-throw, which was where you had to go up to a chalk line and then put your toe on the chalk line and not go over the chalk line and then throw the ball as far as you could throw.

I did.

I won.

It was 1944 and I was ten years old and I was better than all of the other boys at that camp and probably all of the boys everywhere else.

I felt more wonderful than I had ever felt. I felt so thrilled with myself. I felt like God was whispering things to me inside of my head. I felt like God was asking me to have a special secret with him or to have a secret arrangement with him and that I had to keep listening to his secret recommendations inside of my head. I felt like God was telling me to realize that he had made me the most unusual member of the human race and that he was going to need me to be ready for him to go to work for him at any minute for him on whatever thing he said.

They gave me a piece of stiff cloth which was in the shape of a shield and which was in the camp colors and which had five blue stars on it. They said that I was the only boy ever to get a shield with as many as that many stars on it. They said that it was unheard-of for any boy ever to get as many as that many stars on it. But I could already feel that I was forgetting what it felt like to do something which would get you a shield with as many as that many stars on it. I could feel myself forgetting and I could feel everybody else forgetting, even my mother and father and God forgetting. It was just a little while afterwards, but I could tell that everybody was already forgetting everything about it—the head of the camp and the camp counselors and the other campers and the other mothers and the other fathers and my mother and my father and even that I myself was, even though I was trying with all of my might to be the one person who never would.

I felt like God was ashamed of me. I felt like God was sorry that I was the one which he had picked out and that he was getting ready to make a new choice and to choose another boy instead of me and that I had to hurry up before God did it, that I had to be quick about showing him that I could be just as amazing again as I used to be and do something better or at least do something else.

It was August.

I was feeling the strangest feeling that I have ever felt. I was standing there with my parents and with all of the people who had come there for the field day and I was feeling the strangest feeling which I have ever felt.

I felt like lying down on the field. I felt like killing all of the people. I felt like going to sleep and staying asleep until someone came and told me that my parents were dead and that I was all grown up and that there was a new God in heaven and that he liked me better even than the old God had.

My parents kept asking me where did I want to go now and what did I want to do. My parents kept trying to get me to tell them where I thought we should all go now and what was the next thing for us as a family to do. My parents wanted for me to be the one to make up my mind if we should all go someplace special now and what was the best thing for the family, as a family, to do. But I did not know what they meant—do, do, do?

My father took the shield away from me and held it in his hands and kept turning it over and over in his hands and kept looking at the shield and feeling the shield and saying that it was made of buckram and felt. My father kept saying did we know that it was just something which they had put together out of buckram and felt. My father kept saying that the shield was of a very nice quality of buckram and was of a very nice quality of felt but that we should make every effort not to get it wet because it would run all over itself.

I did not know what to do.

I could tell that my parents did not know what to do.

We just stood around and people were going away to all of the vehicles that were going to take them to places and I could tell that we did not know if it was time for us to go.

The head of the camp came over and said that he wanted to shake my hand again and shake the hands of the people who were responsible for giving the Peninsula Athletes Day Camp such an outstanding young individual and such a talented young athlete.

He shook my hand again.

It made me feel dizzy and nearly asleep.

I saw my mother and my father get their hands ready. I saw my father get the shield out of the hand that he thought he was going to need for him to have his hand ready to shake the hand of the head of the camp. I saw my mother take her purse and do the same thing. But the head of the camp just kept shaking my hand, and my mother and my father just kept saying thank you to him, and then the head of the camp let go of my hand and took my father's elbow with one hand and then touched my father on the shoulder with the other hand and then said that we were certainly the very finest of people—and then he went away.

ABOUT THE AUTHOR

At the gravesite
of a friend,
a man is asked
by the rabbi presiding
to say a few words
regarding the deceased.
The man says,
"His brother was worse."